Seagulls from
Copyright © 2022 A:

www.ashleylister.

Published by Chorkie Press August 2022

To Carol-Ann
Your review made
me blush.
Thankyou

The Seagull Has Landed

The sign said: *Welcome to Blackpool*. With a lowering thundercloud on the horizon, and the first flecks of rain coming down, the view did not look particularly welcoming. The famous tower was a faraway blimp on the horizon. The curves of a gigantic rollercoaster loomed like the curls of loose threads near the hem of a threadbare grey sky. The whole scene looked even less welcoming when a hefty spatter of seagull shit slapped across the windscreen. The guano appeared like a mixture of white emulsion with a green and yellow kernel at its heart.

Overhead a seagull screamed.

"Filthy fucking creatures," Chris grumbled. He hit the wiper and the screen wash. For a moment the entire screen was whitened by diluted bird shit. Then the car's single blade began to clear the mess and he was looking at the approaching town of Blackpool and telling himself this weekend wouldn't be as bad as he feared.

"Isn't it supposed to be lucky?" Pamela asked.

Chris said nothing. The car was a Pagani Huayra Roadster, based on the classic styling of the Pagani Zonda R. It was the sort of glossy, low-riding sports car that made heads turn when he drove past. The Nero Blackstar paintwork was something he polished every week until the vehicle was back to its usual oily lustre. A spattering of corrosive seagull crap on the bonnet was going to mean he needed to T-cut the damned thing over the next weekend or maybe shell out for a professional external valet. If that was needed, he'd be looking at a bill in excess of two hundred quid just to remove the stain from a spatter of bird shit. In short: Chris didn't feel particularly lucky.

"Bloody gulls," he muttered.

"But isn't it supposed to be lucky?" Pam pressed.

He tightened his facial muscles, hoping it looked like he was giving the dizzy bitch a grin whilst he nodded. A weekend with Pam promised several good things. For a start, because she'd selected Blackpool, he knew she was cheap. Also, she banged like a shithouse door in a thunderstorm. And, probably most important for his needs, she was very, very attractive. Her hair, breasts, legs and face all seemed pleasingly proportioned, youthful, and made her strikingly similar to the stars of his favourite clips on Pornhub. If only he'd been able to mute her volume in the same way he could mute a Pornhub clip when the woman had one of those fake screeching orgasms, Pam would have been the ideal partner. Maddeningly, Pam seemed to take exception to his attempts to cover her lips whilst they were having sex. And, after he'd tried it once, she was adamant he couldn't stuff her knickers in her mouth ever again.

Another spatter of seagull shit was thrown across the windscreen. It was a torrential downpour of seagull shit, he thought miserably. "Bastard things," he snapped.

As they'd been driving, Chris had noticed the screech of the seagulls increase the closer they got to Blackpool. At first it had been a faraway sound, slightly jarring and a little discordant, but nothing more than a reminder that they were nearing the coast. A few miles closer and he realised he wasn't hearing the gentle seagulls that could be heard cooing over the intro of *The Sleepy Lagoon* when it was played on *Desert Island Discs*. These were gulls that were screeching for food or territory or sex. After a while he'd wondered if he was really hearing gulls, or if he was approaching some nightmare location where babies and infants were being massacred, mutilated and flayed alive. The cries of the gulls were loud, almost human, and chilling with their shrill and piercing wail. He didn't want to think it sounded like peeled babies being dipped in vinegar, but once that image was fixed in his thoughts, it refused to go.

He hit the screen wash and the Roadster's single wiper made short work of the popshot of seagull cream that had covered the windscreen. Chris tried not to notice that the edges of the screen were now daubed with white lines as reminders of what had stained the vehicle.

"What do you want to do first once we've checked in?" Pamela asked.

Chris waggled a suggestive eyebrow. "Do you really need to ask what I want to do?"

Pam groaned good-naturedly and punched him lightly on the arm. "We didn't just come here to do *that*, did we?" she admonished.

He shrugged, genuinely puzzled by her comment. "We're staying at the Cleveleys Hotel just outside Blackpool," he reminded her. "Aside from watching the traffic lights change, I don't think there's much else to do."

Pam giggled and shook her head. The conversation continued as they parked in front of their hotel and walked hurriedly to the reception desk trying to avoid the fattening droplets of rain that were falling from the darkening skies. Whilst Chris summoned the concierge by slamming repeatedly on the bell, Pam said, "I think I'd like to go for a run before we have our meal this evening."

"A run?" Chris echoed. He said the word with the same lack of comprehension he would have used if she'd said she wanted to go for a chocolate bison or an electric handshake. The option of going for 'a run' simply made no sense and he stared at her curiously as his head shook slowly from side to side.

Pam gestured at her clothes, a bright orange and black designer-wear exercise outfit from the brand Axis. "I'm already in my running gear," she explained. "It would be silly not to take advantage of the opportunity."

"But it's about to piss it down," Chris objected.

"A little rain never hurt anyone," she laughed easily.

Chris stopped himself from mentioning the people who had recently died in floods in Europe, or asking what happened to the people who lived next door to Noah. Instead, he said, "I'm going to get myself a massive bourbon and chillax whilst you're out running in the rain."

The concierge approached. He was a broad-faced man with a patient smile and a massive stomach. His once-white shirtsleeves were rolled up to reveal brawny forearms and a fading tattoo that had probably been an anchor. He had been grinning genially as he stepped behind the reception desk, but he frowned on hearing Chris's words. Glancing from Chris to Pam he said, "Was one of you thinking of going out running? Are you sure that's wise?"

"This is what I was saying," Chris agreed. "It's about to chuck it down, isn't it?"

The concierge nodded uncomfortably. "Yes, Sir," he agreed. "That's just the point I was going to make."

Chris wasn't sure he believed this. He got the impression that there was something else on the concierge's mind, but he couldn't think of a way to press his point without sounding either paranoid or mental.

"I'm just going to do 5K along the seafront," Pam said firmly.

Chris could tell, from the determination in her voice, that she was now intent on going for her run, regardless of how bad the weather got or how much common sense was thrust on her. He had met plenty of women with the defiant attitude of doing exactly the opposite of what better minds advised. He supposed one of the reasons he had ended up in bed with so many of such types of stubborn-minded women was simply because their more perceptive female friends had warned them against him and those stubborn-minded women had dated Chris as a show of defiance. In some circles, he suspected, he was likely a cautionary tale. The thought made him grin as though, in acquiring infamy, he'd achieved something.

"It'll be dark by the time you set off," the concierge told her.

"I've got good night vision," Pam returned.

"And I'd strongly advise against running along the seafront after dark," the concierge said. He'd lowered his tone to a grave whisper as he added, "There have been *incidents*." He said the final word with the sort of stress people used for the most delicate of euphemisms. This was the same way someone talked about an elderly racist relative as having *old-fashioned* opinions. Or a closeted celebrity having a *special* male friend.

"What sort of incidents?" Pam asked.

The concierge shook his head, called for a porter and said, "I don't want to sour the start of your stay with us by sharing scary stories. Please, just trust me when I say, running along the seafront after dark is not advised."

"OK," Pam said simply. "Thanks for the warning."

And Chris could hear, in her tone, that she was going to ignore the advice and run along the seafront anyway. Secretly, he hoped that one of her sensible girlfriends had warned Pam not to do anal with him.

★

Forty minutes later Chris was sitting in his room and the first stirrings of panic began to flutter in his breast. He was on his third JD and Coke, peering out of the hotel window to the storm-lashed seafront, and wondering what the hell had happened to Pam. She had gone out for her run, promising him that she would do 5K at the most, but that was forty minutes ago. Her typical 5K time, when she was feeling competitive, came in well under twenty minutes. He had never known her take longer than thirty minutes to do such a distance. And here it was, forty full minutes since she'd set off, and he felt a growing disquiet that he wasn't going to see her again.

Worse: it was impossible to think clearly with the murdered-baby screech he was hearing from the gulls outside the hotel. The cries were horrific. They were the agonised wails of the tortured souls hurled into Hell's fiery pits. They were the brutalised screams of torment and agony he would have expected to hear if someone had thrown a rabid werewolf into a convent. It was the sound that would come if a hook-handed rapist broke into a girls' dormitory. The birds did not chirrup, or tweet or trill or quack or do anything that had a remotely musical sound. The bloody gulls squawked as though they had human voice boxes and were suffering at the hands of a sadistic murderer.

"Where the fuck are you, Pam?" Chris grumbled.

He drained his JD and Coke and poured himself another one. If she didn't get back soon he figured he would be too pissed to take advantage of her lax morals and Pornhub good looks, but a growing sense of unease wouldn't let him steer clear of the drink. He needed the alcohol so he didn't have to think about what might have happened to her. She'd gone for a run on the seafront. And, according to the concierge, the seafront was where there had been *incidents*.

After sixty minutes he tried ringing her mobile.

She always took her Samsung with her when she went running. The GPS tracked her location and, because she wore earbuds with it, he figured she could answer a call without interrupting her run.

The connection went straight through to voicemail.

It was ninety minutes after she'd left to run when he called down to the reception desk and asked if Pam had left a message for him.

"I'm sorry, Sir," the concierge said coolly. "We've had no message. And your lady friend was warned not to-"

Chris hung up, unwilling to hear the Blackpool version of 'I told you so' from the concierge. He tried to think what might have happened to Pam but it was difficult to concentrate because of a mixture of JD, driving rain against his hotel window and screeching seagulls. A decent guy, he supposed, would possibly go out into the streets and look for her.

But that would have meant leaving behind his bourbon and the warmth of this room and getting piss-wet through for a dumb bitch too stupid not to go running in the rain and the dark. Coming to a quick decision, he drained his fifth bourbon, staggered to the doorway, and then took a lift downstairs to the hotel restaurant.

★

"Are you dining alone?" the waitress asked.

"Unless you'd care to join me," Chris said. The words were slightly slurred but he could still tell that she was impressed. "I'm the guest with the Pagani," he added, giving her a conspiratorial wink. He held up his key fob which was shaped like a shiny Pagani Roadster.

The waitress ignored the key fob and smiled sympathetically. "That Pagani must be very uncomfortable," she told him. "Would you like me to get a doughnut so your chair's a little more comfortable?"

He puzzled his way through her words before realising she'd made a mistake. "No," he said hurriedly. "The Pagani Roadster is a sports car: not another name for haemorrhoids." He was still trying to assure her of this point when she left him alone at his table, studying the menu and wondering how he had ended up wasting his weekend on his own in Blackpool with a date that had gone AWOL.

And not just any date. She'd been a Pornhub lookalike with a reputation that said she was easier than a tabloid crossword. She'd been a dead cert and he'd been looking forward to a weekend of alcohol and sex. But now, unless he could convince the waitress that he didn't have haemorrhoids, Chris could see he was just going to

8

spend the night wanking himself to sleep whilst he cried about his loneliness.

It wasn't fair, he thought bitterly. He owned a Pagani Roadster.

"Excuse me, Sir." It was the concierge who had spoken. He appeared at Chris's side like the shopkeeper in the old Mr Ben cartoons. The concierge was holding a padded cushion that looked like a doughnut. "Your waitress said you might be able to make use of this."

"No," Chris said firmly. "I think we were talking at cross-purposes."

The concierge glanced at the empty seat facing Chris and then said, "Your companion hasn't yet returned from her short run."

"No," Chris said again. This time he could feel anger tightening the word in his throat.

"Perhaps I can help with that," the concierge said brightly. "I think I might know where you can find her. Would you like to follow me through the kitchens?"

It wasn't what Chris was expecting to hear but he figured there must be a reason for the concierge to make such an invitation. He stood up, didn't bother objecting when the concierge placed the padded doughnut on his chair, and followed obediently as the man led him to a doorway marked STAFF ONLY.

The noise in the kitchens was not what Chris had been expecting. Aside from the hiss and sizzle of cooking food, the flurry of warm baking flavours, and the chatter and banter of chefs, he could hear the nearby screech of gulls as they tried to outdo each other with their menacing cries. This was the sound a baby would make if some stuck a knife its eye. This was the sound a Toddler would make if someone cut it with a rusty razor. This was the sound a young girl would make if she was beaten, battered and sexually brutalised.

"Those birds are fucking loud," Chris told the concierge.

"The kitchen doors are open," the concierge explained. He raised his voice to make himself heard over the noise. "And the gulls have a habit of congregating around local kitchens. They're seldom quiet when they're feeding."

He continued walking through the kitchen, heading toward the open doorway. A hiss of rain was audible beneath the screech of the cacophonic birdsong. Chris could hear the dry flap and flutter of wings, the sounds punctuating the screams and squeals of each cry from a gull.

"Just through there, Sir," the concierge said quietly, gesturing for Chris to step outside.

Puzzled, Chris did as the concierge suggested.

"What am I doing out here?" Chris asked.

"You'll find your companion out there," the concierge explained. And then he closed the door.

Chris found himself alone in the yard behind the kitchen, listening to the screech and scream of a dozen fat gulls. Light from a nearby streetlamp illuminated the grey and white plumage of the birds, as well as the falling silver needles of rain. He could see oily black bin bags on the floor and two aggressive birds were fighting over them. But that wasn't the sight that captured his attention.

He could see the remains of Pam's body sprawled beside one of the bins.

It was her orange and black Axis running gear he recognised first. A seagull was pecking at the remnants of her face. It's beak and head were sticky with blood. A gristle-like piece of flesh hung from the side of its mouth. Whilst it continued to peck at its meal, it considered Chris with a blank-eyed expression of malice that seemed to say, "You're next."

Several of the gulls were working on Pam's body. She had a missing arm and there was a hole in her throat. The squawking birds occasionally snapped at each other for a choicer piece of meat. But, for the majority of the time, they seemed happy to screech like banshees and then continue to feed from their victim.

Chris turned to the closed kitchen door.

There was no handle.

He hammered his fist against the door and called, "Let me in. You have to let me in. There's a dead woman out here and she's been killed and eaten by these bloody gulls."

From behind the door he heard a laconic chuckle. Speaking carefully, the concierge said, "We know what's out there. Your companion was one of the two offerings we've made to the gulls this evening."

"Two offerings?" Chris asked doubtfully. "What's the other one?"

Something flapped against the side of his head. He flipped out a hand, to push it away and half-turned. A beak pushed at his eye and plucked it from its socket. The pain was so enormous he fell to his knees with a squeal that sounded as though it had come from the birds. And then they were on him: fluttering, flapping, pecking and snapping.

And, in that moment, Chris understood that he was the other offering.

The Punch and Jodie Show

The Blackpool illuminations were bright enough to darken the night sky to inky impenetrability. Because of the light-pollution there was no visible moon above and there wouldn't be stars again until the end of the summer season. Deacon and Cheryl, lurking behind the Bispham tableaux at the northernmost end of the promenade, were swathed in discreet shadows only yards away from the chitter-chatter of excited conversations coming from those standing on the lit side of the promenade. It was a Wednesday night, with a chilly wind blowing in from the sea and virtually howling when it reached the clifftops, and Deacon and Cheryl had just finished a brisk but effective outdoor fuck.

"Isn't this romantic?" Cheryl asked, squeezing his hand after pulling her knickers back up.

She was tall and blonde and, save for a slight tummy, she had a relatively athletic body on her. Deacon had thought she might be out of his league when he'd first seen her, but she'd accepted his invitation for a walk on the promenade and, when he'd made the lewd suggestion that they could do more behind the tableaus, she had proved to be more than amenable. He supposed it was that easiness she had displayed that was now making him wonder if he was really attracted to her.

"Don't you think it's romantic?" Cheryl asked again.

Deacon shrugged. He wouldn't have called it romantic. He'd got a knee-trembler from a slapper at the top of the cliffs. The wind was so bad it felt like it had blown enough sand up his arsehole so he'd be shitting dunes for the next month. But he knew better than to voice such opinions in response to a question about the romance of the evening. Experience had taught him that even slappers with the lax morals of Cheryl had feelings.

"Do you want to come and do something fun?" he asked suddenly.

"More fun than what we just did?" Cheryl sounded doubtful.

Deacon laughed and wondered if he was supposed to make some comment about how great the sex had been. It hadn't been anything remarkable. A shag on the prom was no more extraordinary than finding a Blackpool shop selling fish and chips, or Blackpool rock, or cheap dildoes. Given Cheryl's unenthusiastic performance, sloppy kisses flavoured with Lambrini and a fanny that had clearly seen more cock than Colonel Sanders, Deacon was hard pushed to think of it as fun rather than an expected chore to prove his masculinity.

Taking her hand, pulling her with him as they descended into darkness along one of the pathways leading down the cliff to the sea defences above the seashore, Deacon said, "I promise you, this is going to be the most exciting thing you've ever done in Blackpool."

"Ooh!" she giggled. "Where are you taking me?"

He called the words over his shoulder as they ran down a slope that submerged them in shadows. The cliffs were crisscrossed with sloping paths that led up and down from the clifftops to the sea defences above the beach. Descending the path in the darkness, whilst hurrying at speed, was a breath-taking experience. Deacon had often thought it was like running into the unknown: hurtling into oblivion. Even though he could see a wink of torchlight on the beach below, it still felt as though he was throwing himself down into the blackness of an unseen and unforgiving hell.

"You're not a local, are you?" he called to her.

"No."

"So, you don't know about the problems that Blackpool has?"

"Problems?"

"Blackpool has problems with poverty," he began.

"Poverty?" she resisted him for a moment and said, "You're not some sort of social worker, are you?"

He laughed, amused by the thought. "The town has problems with poverty," he explained. "This means we have a large homeless population and we have lots of chemical dependency."

"Do you mean drugs?"

"Yeah. I mean drugs. Have you never seen any of the YouTube videos where someone feeds K2 to a local spice-head?"

There was a moment's pause before she said, "Yeah. I've seen a couple of those." She was silent for another beat before saying, "They're hilarious."

He chuckled and said, "Yeah. I've filmed a couple of those myself."

"Legend," she laughed happily. When he began to run again, she followed him with more enthusiasm. "Is that where we're going, now?" she asked eagerly. "Are we going to feed a spice-head?"

"No. We've got something better than that to do. We're going to go and see the Punch and Jodie Show."

He could sense that she was frowning, not sure if she'd heard him correctly and trying to make sense of his words as he spat them back at her. She was still running after him, her Primark heels clipping on the stone steps as they hurried from the top of the cliffs to the brutalist concrete walkway of the sea defences that edged the seashore.

The darkness here was like swimming in black paint. Occasional glimpses of torchlight on the beach assured Deacon he was going in the right direction, but his vision remained sufficiently clouded by the night's shadows for him to doubt his senses. Even when they were climbing down the stone stairs that led to the sandy shore, he was still unsure that he was going to find the Punch and Jodie Show.

But he didn't let Cheryl see his reservations.

The air was acidic with the fishy stench of brine. He could feel the gritty texture of sand between the soles of his trainers and the long stone steps. Deacon cautioned himself to slow down for fear of stumbling in the dark. A cold wind slid smoothly from the Irish Sea, its chilly fingers caressing Deacon's face and neck and making him shiver.

"Is somebody burning something down there?" Cheryl asked. "Are those candles I can see?"

He laughed and shook his head. Reaching back for her, taking her hand and guiding her onto the beach he said, "Those aren't candles. They're tiki torches." He allowed her eyes to adjust to the view, figuring it would take a moment to get used to the sight of a circle of eight torches burning on the damp sand.

"What's going on?" Cheryl asked doubtfully.

She had paused at the bottom of the steps and no longer seemed eager to rush with him into the darkness of this adventure. He wondered if she had seen some of the dark figures moving near the torches, or if she was just picking up the irresistible idea that something was wrong down here. Very wrong.

"Is there really a Punch and Judy show down here?"

"Punch and Jodie," he corrected. He pulled gently on her hand, and with obvious reluctance, she stumbled along after him toward the torchlight. "Punch and Jodie is the local name for this piece of seaside entertainment," Deacon explained. "I think, when I've seen it happening elsewhere in the country, they simply call it hobo-fighting."

She gasped as her eyes adjusted slowly to the dim light and Deacon could understand her reaction. In the centre of the circle of tiki torches stood two tramps: both shirtless, with their hands bandaged. Even in this dim light it was obvious that they were both homeless. They wore beards that looked to be competing for being straggliest and most unkempt. The orange and yellow torchlight fluttering across their bodies showed flesh that was either bruised by dirt, injury or poor life choices. The pants they wore, saggy-arsed sweatpants that were overstretched at the knees, were ill-fitting and tied with string at the waist. But it was also clear that both participants had formidable builds. Admittedly, they were more dadbod than ripped or jacked. But each had a decent set of biceps and pecs and both looked more than capable of handling a physical confrontation.

"They're genuine hobos," Cheryl gasped.

"Hence the reason they call this hobo-fighting," Deacon agreed.

A crowd of two or three dozen people stood around them, some of them chattering happily whilst others looked to be involved in making bets. The light wasn't great around those making bets, but it was bright enough for Deacon to see substantial wads of money changing hands. He checked his wallet and wondered if it was worth putting a ton on Jodie's main player.

Cheryl clutched tight at his arm and whispered in his ear, "Is this really hobo-fighting? Is that what we're going to watch?"

Deacon stepped closer to the circle and, seeing a figure he recognised, handed over two fifty pound notes. "Two to watch the match," he explained.

"Will you be having a bet on tonight's game, Deacon?"

Cheryl arched her eyebrows, as though she was surprised to hear it was a woman's voice. The figure was wrapped in shapeless clothes with a black baseball cap concealing her eyes and a hoodie pulled over her baseball cap. Deacon, who had met Jodie in places other than at the hobo fights, remembered the woman constantly wore black: from her jet-black trainers and jeans, through to her jet-black sweatshirt and hair. The two fifties Jodie held had disappeared and the woman was shifting rhythmically from side to side as she waited for Deacon's answer to her question.

"Who's your fighter?" Deacon asked.

"Raging Bill," Jodie said coolly. She nodded toward the illuminated ring and Cheryl saw two tramps standing there. "Bill's the one with the X on his tit."

Cheryl peered into the darkness and saw that the sandy-haired tramp with the straggly beard had a letter X branded over his left breast. The skin was puckered into a raised bump that looked painful and slightly infected. The other competitor, bald and less imposing, had a freshly branded letter O in the same place. Cheryl figured this was how the fighters were going to be identified for those unfamiliar with their distinguishing features.

"Raging Bill?" Deacon marvelled. "Is this his third fight or his fourth?"

"Eighth," Jodie said. "He's been undefeated for the past month."

"Impressive," Deacon muttered. "And his opponent?"

Jodie shrugged. "A couple of Preston lads have brought him down as a contender." Lowering her voice she said, "He doesn't stand a chance. He's got the build. But there's no fight in him. They're pitching him here under the nickname Hulk Hobo and that's the best thing about him."

Deacon laughed. He produced his wallet and took out a sheaf of banknotes. "A grand on Raging Bill to win," he said, pushing the money into Jodie's hand. He made sure that Cheryl could see he was gambling with a substantial amount of cash. He knew he no longer needed to impress the woman but force of habit made him try to flash the cash so she could see he was a man of means.

Jodie nodded agreement to Deacon's bet and made the money disappear into one of her many black pockets. She glanced beyond him and Deacon understood that she was checking to see if anyone else was going to be coming to watch the match. When she nodded her head, making an indistinct gesture to someone neither Cheryl nor Deacon could see, an expectant silence fell over those gathered and they knew the match was about to start. The only noises came from the hiss of the nearby sea, as it headed lazily toward them, and the faraway roar of traffic from beyond the cliff tops.

Jodie stepped into the illuminated circle and raised a hand. "Ladies and gentlemen," she called. She turned 360^0 so that none of the audience felt excluded. "Thank you for coming to tonight's game. I trust you've all paid your admission fees and made suitable bets." She paused for a moment in case a member of the audience wanted to offer her more money or make an additional wager.

No one spoke but Cheryl was practically squirming next to Deacon and he could understand why. The tension in the air was growing richer and more electric as the event got closer to beginning. Deacon could feel his own heartbeat hammering with increased excitement as he realised he was going to be watching an illicit fight and he knew it would be a deathmatch.

"Is this like bare knuckle fighting?" Cheryl asked, whispering the words on hot breath against the cold shell of his ear.

"Not exactly," Deacon said, pointing to the fighters. Both men had their hands clumsily bandaged until it looked like they were wearing balloons on the ends of their wrists. The white bandages were crisscrossed by grey lines that had a dull metallic glint in the glare of the tiki torch light.

"Tonight's competitors are local boy, Raging Bill: undefeated winner of the last eight matches…" Jodie paused for a moment, allowing a handful of audience members to applaud and shout encouragement. "And he'll be fighting against our esteemed visitor from Preston, Mr Hulk Hobo."

The cheers for Hulk Hobo were louder but, like everyone else at the match, Hulk Hobo clearly knew the smart money was against him. No one got to be undefeated champion over eight matches without having some serious fighting skills. Hulk Hobo eyed his competitor warily, his sharp eyes looking for some potential weakness he could exploit.

"Please remember," Jodie told her audience. "These two gentlemen of the road are going to fight each other to the death."

Hulk Hobo, the tramp marked by the letter O on his chest, widened his eyes in surprise and shook his head. "I'm not fighting no one to the death." He raised one bandaged hand and pointed it at Raging Bill. "I'll beat the fucker unconscious but I'm not killing him."

Jodie turned to the two Preston lads who had brought Hulk Hobo to the match. "Did you not tell your boy about the rules?"

They wore matching beanie caps and lurked in the shadows sharing a spliff. The taller one was wearing a dark tracksuit. The shorter one was wearing jeans and a tired denim jacket. "We didn't want to make our boy nervous," the one in the tracksuit called.

"We thought he'd enjoy the surprise," the other added. They both erupted into the spluttering giggles of a pair of stoners.

Hulk Hobo's features dissolved into an expression of pained misery.

Jodie turned to the fighter and said, "I've got some bad news for you, son. You'll be involved in a fight to the death. But you don't have to worry about killing your opponent. With your attitude, you'll clearly be the loser."

"I'm not fighting no one to the death," Hulk Hobo insisted.

Jodie nodded and stepped out of the ring. "To the death!" she called loudly.

The audience picked up her chant and called, "To the death!"

Raging Bill stepped close to Hulk Hobo who was waving his arms in a gesture that indicated he didn't want to participate. Because his hands were completely hidden by the white bandages his gestures looked clumsy and inarticulate. He looked like a runway controller trying to express a complex argument as he backed away.

"I'm not fighting you to death," he told Bill.

"Are they really going to kill each other?" Cheryl whispered.

"One of them will kill the other," Deacon promised. "They don't have a choice," he explained. "This fight has been planned for the past week and the players don't get a say as to whether or not they are willing participants. All they can do is fight to the death." He nodded into the illuminated ring and said, "Look at the way their hands are bandaged. Do you notice anything odd about it?"

Cheryl squinted at the pair for a moment and then gasped with horror. The stiff white bandages were tight and so thick they looked cartoonish. But they were bound by metallic wires and, as Cheryl studied them her eyes opened wide.

"Is that barbwire?" she asked.

Deacon nodded. "Exactly." Lengths of barbwire had been looped and twisted around each fighter's bound fists and up their bound forearms. Both fighters were going into the arena wearing barbwire boxing gauntlets.

"Why are they wearing barbwire?" Cheryl asked.

"Does your single brain cell ever get lonely?" he wondered. He kept the thought to himself. "In cock-fighting," Deacon explained, "They get the cocks to kill one another by fixing razors to their feet. This means, even if the cocks are reluctant to fight to the death, like Hulk Hobo here, they're sufficiently armed to do a shitload of damage." He nodded at the barbwire bindings and cutthroat razors on the bound hands of the tramps and said, "This is the same principle."

"They're really going to fight each other to the death?" Cheryl said. There was a breathless excitement in her voice that showed she was unable to disguise her enthusiasm. "I didn't think such things happened in this country. Are they really fighting to the death?"

"Yes," said Deacon.

"No," Hulk Hobo said firmly. He responded as though he'd been listening to Cheryl's whispered concerns. "I'm not fighting to the death," he insisted. He took a step away from Raging Bill as the opponent pressed closer. "I didn't sign up for a deathmatch and I'm not participating."

"That's going to make it easier for me," Raging Bill announced, swinging a haymaker at Hulk Hobo and catching the side of his face. The barbs on Bill's glove gouged a series of bloody lines on his opponent's face and ripped through the tangle of straggly beard that hung from his chin.

Hulk Hobo roared with discomfort and staggered backwards. "You fucking idiot," he exclaimed. "Don't you see you're playing into their hands? If we don't fight each other, what are these pussies going to do?"

"If we both refuse, they'll be burying two corpses tonight," Bill grunted. Before he had finished saying the words, Raging Bill used his right fist to attempt an uppercut.

Hulk Hobo blocked the assault with a defensive sideswipe. It meant his left forearm was abraded by a rush of minor lacerations, but he protected his face from the wicked glint of the razor and the brutal thrust of the barbwire. Maddeningly, the sideswipe left Hulk Hobo defenceless against an unexpected jab from Raging Bill's southpaw. The blow was hard against the side of Hulk Hobo's head and the added impact of the barbs on Bill's knuckles made him scream. A flap of skin was torn from his mouth and a phlegmy string of blood spilled from Hulk Hobo's face.

"Will you stop doing that?" Hulk Hobo demanded. He sounded furious. "Didn't you hear what I said, you fucking idiot? Fighting each other is just playing into their hands. Are you too stupid to realise that?"

Raging Bill slammed a cross into Hulk's left kidney. "I might be stupid," he admitted. "But I'm not the one bringing pacifism to a deathmatch."

Two more punches and it was all but finished. Raging Bill aimed a lead hook at the right side of Hulk Hobo's face. It was a powerhouse blow that would have left him concussed if it had connected. Hulk stepped back, dodging the force of the punch, but he didn't step back far enough. The bracelets of barbwire that covered Bill's bandaged forearms brushed past Hulk's face and tore through his nose.

Hulk screamed, a sound that spluttered wetly through a combination of tears and rushing blood and unexpected pain. Bill took advantage of the situation and slammed a forceful jab into Hulk Hobo's throat. The contender went down on his knees, choking for air and waving a futile hand to indicate submission.

"Finish him," Jodie called.

Raging Bill drove a vicious kick into Hulk Hobo's chest.

"Isn't kicking against the rules?" Cheryl asked Deacon.

"This is an unlicensed hobo deathmatch," Deacon reminded her. "They're wearing barbwire gloves with razorblade accoutrements, and it's one continuous round until the loser has stopped breathing. I don't think any of them will be worrying about rules such as kicking."

"Finish him," Jodie insisted.

Hulk Hobo lay sprawled with his back on the wet sand, his battered and bloody face looking red as he strove to get air into his lungs. Raging Bill settled himself over the man and began to rain punches down on him with blow after blow of uncompromising force. Hulk moaned with the first three punches but, after those, he remained peculiarly silent. After a minute of pummelling his opponent, Raging Bill stood up, held his gloved and bound hands in the air, and shook with victorious jubilation.

A crackle of something rang through the night. Raging Bill roared and fell to the floor and Deacon saw a pair of sizzling cables protruding from the triumphant fighter's back.

"What the fuck?" Cheryl exclaimed, squeezing tight at Deacon's bicep.

"Taser," Deacon said coolly. "Jodie knows she can't trust her reigning champion to simply go back to his cage and wait for the next match. It's easier to tase him, take the bindings off his hands, and then put him back in the cage until she's organised the next match."

As they watched, two of Jodie's assistants, an enormous black man and a muscly young woman wearing combat gear, walked toward Raging Bill and used wire snips to remove the barbwire gloves from his hands. Behind them Jodie was taking money from the Preston guys in beanie hats whilst two of her other assistants were dragging Hulk Hobo toward a Transit van parked atop the sand. A tall figure approached Deacon and thrust a wodge of money into his hands.

"Your winnings," he explained. "Jodie says she'll see you at the next event in a week's time."

"That was incredible," Cheryl told Deacon. The excitement in her voice was so rich it was almost palpable. "I've never seen anything so exciting. Can I come with you to the next fight? Can we make this a regular thing for you and me?"

Deacon considered this and found himself coming to a swift decision. Cheryl was OK in the looks department, and she gave a good knee-trembler. But she was proving to be a damned sight more clingy than he needed. It wasn't that he had another girlfriend waiting in the wings, or that he believed he could attract someone better. He just didn't want to form a relationship with someone as shallow as Cheryl.

"You enjoyed that?" Deacon asked, forcing his features into a pleasant grin. He placed a hand on the tall figure's arm making him wait with them for a moment. "Just wait until you see what's Jodie has lined up for Friday night entertainment," Deacon told Cheryl.

"What is it?" she asked eagerly.

He placed a finger over his lips as though indicating it was a secret and then turned to the tall figure. "Is Jodie still running slapper fights?"

When the tall figure nodded, Deacon snaked an arm around Cheryl's waist. She tried to pull away from him, clearly understanding what he had planned for her, but it was already too late.

Gym'll Fix It

Dave usually found the treadmill relaxing: but not today. It was early Friday morning and, as a regular at The Gym on Talbot Road, he was familiar with the positives and negatives of his chosen fitness venue. The price was affordable. The range of equipment was substantial, and most pieces of kit worked effectively. Importantly, the 24/7 opening hours meant that he could work out at a time that suited him, rather than having to wait for someone else's schedule.

Of course, there were also drawbacks.

Getting to the gym in the early hours meant wading through a traffic of hobos, hookers and pisstags, any of which could take the pleasant shine from the start of the day. Sometimes it meant driving through flocks of seagulls that were fighting over discarded bags of rubbish that they'd dragged into the middle of the roads with their clumsy attempts to get to the good stuff inside. Sometimes it meant driving over the carcasses of roadkill seagulls that hadn't been swift enough to get out of the way of an oncoming vehicle.

Once inside the gym, Dave also didn't like it when any other gym members tried talking to him: he was there to exercise muscles other than his jaw. He didn't like the headache-inducing thump of the 'music' that was so loud it managed to drone through his noise-cancelling headphones. And he didn't like the huge windows that surrounded the gym and allowed every passing pedestrian a chance to peer in and take the piss if they fancied whilst he was running a treadmill.

There was a pedestrian staring at him this morning and he figured, from the guy's poor dress sense and the way he swayed whilst standing, the man was probably homeless and possibly off his tits on cheap alcohol or some budget concoction of horse tranquiliser and garden fertiliser. Behind him was a gaggle of five seagulls waving their wings territorially and screeching at each other as they all tried to claim ownership of a discarded McDonald's burger box. It was a surreal situation with Dave running toward the plate glass window at a constant speed of 10K per hour, and the homeless guy standing in front of him, swaying drunkenly, and pointing and laughing.

Dave flipped the guy a finger.

The homeless guy cackled soundlessly. With his mouth open he revealed sore gums, black stumps of yellowing teeth and what looked like a cancerous spot on the back of his soft palate. Any sympathy Dave had for him was immediately banished when the homeless guy began to run on the spot in a cruel and rather unnecessary parody of Dave's unsophisticated gait.

Dave wasn't a professional runner and it was easy for him to feel self-conscious. He used the treadmill to try and address the slight paunch that made his 36" waist pants feel tight and restrictive. He occasionally used the weights in an optimistic bid to transform his moobers into pecs. But he refused to show his embarrassment in light of the unwarranted parody he was enduring.

The homeless guy ran with a ridiculous waddle for a few moments before pointing a finger at Dave so the message was clear: I'm running like an arsehole because that's how you run.

This time, Dave didn't flip him off. Without breaking his speed, and continuing to maintain his respectable 10K pace, he moved his fist back and forth a couple of times in the international sign of masturbation. Then he pointed at the homeless guy to underline what the mime was supposed to mean: you're a wanker.

The homeless guy accepted this with indifference. He had clearly been called far worse during his time. He hawked a wad of snot onto the floor at his feet, scratched at his balls, and then began to perform his parody run again. This time he added to the performance. Aside from the shambling run, the homeless guy gestured to show a swollen belly. He mimed someone running in a state of breathlessness that possibly suggested angina or emphysema. He even, for some reason Dave couldn't fathom, held his little finger at crotch level and made a couple of rather lame gestures with it. To complete the mime he pointed at Dave so his message could be fully understood: you run like an arsehole, you're fat, you're out of shape, and I suspect your penis is incredibly small.

Dave stopped running. He put his feet on the edges of the treadmill and allowed the rubber platform to continue spinning between his open legs whilst he glared fixedly at the homeless guy.

Not letting his gaze shift from the man's face, Dave pulled out the pockets of his sweatpants to show they were empty. Then he pointed at the homeless guy. He hoped the message was clear: call me all the names you want – you're still the one who's got no money.

A smile crossed his lips when he saw the homeless guy spit an angry curse at him and then march away into the slowly blossoming dawn. He was still grinning to himself when he lurched back onto the treadmill and resumed his 10k per hour pace. The fighting seagulls had gone and one of them had taken the burger box. All that remained to show they'd ever been there was a spatter of runny white droppings marking the centre of the road.

Dave's phone rang shrilly through his headphones. He lifted his wrist and read the caller ID on his Fitbit: UNKNOWN CALLER. In his line of work it was not uncommon to get calls from strangers and he tapped the button on the headphones answering the call and waiting for the caller to speak.

"I'm looking for a guy called Dave."

"You've found one," Dave told him. He tried to keep the exertion from his voice but it wasn't easy whilst he was running. According to the timer on the treadmill he'd been running for a little over forty-five minutes and, according to the distance meter, he was almost up to the 8K mark.

"I've been told you can find people," the caller explained.

"Who are you looking for?"

"My brother's gone missing. We'd heard reports he might have been seen in the Blackpool area. I figured, with you being based there, you might be able to help."

"How long has he been missing?"

"It's been a month now."

"Email me a recent photo of him," Dave said, putting his feet on either side of the treadmill and allowing the rubber to spin as he rested for a moment. "Include a phone number and any salient details and I'll get back to you before the end of the day to say whether or not I can do anything."

"You think you might be able to locate him?"

He hated hearing the hope in the caller's voice. There had been too many times in the past when he'd heard that note of desperation from someone yearning to see light at the end of a bleak tunnel. It was a tone of voice that made him feel as though he was expected to give substance to blind optimism, but he'd disappointed enough clients in the past to be cautious about giving false promises. Taking a deep breath, and launching himself more swiftly onto the treadmill, Dave said, "Send me a photo, and all the information you've got, and I'll get back to you before the end of the day."

Gulls Just Want to Have Fun

Kitty Wakes waited at the Cleveleys Hotel reception desk, strumming long talon-like fingernails against the desk and idly admiring her reflection in the full-length mirror that sat beside the hotel's staircase. She was wearing a three-quarter length coat. The arms, hood and breast were a brilliant white whilst the design on the back incorporated a smoky-grey feather pattern that darkened from pale at the collar to charcoal toward the hem. Kitty was waiting for the concierge to keep an appointment with her and, as was usual for the scruffy, fat fucker, he was late for their scheduled meeting. Not that Kitty minded. She enjoyed people-watching and that was something she could do effectively at the hotel reception desk.

The Cleveleys Hotel overlooked the seafront and allowed those gathered in the bar to watch lazy orange sunsets descending over the tranquillity of the Irish Sea. It was early evening and the air in the hotel was seasoned with the heady scents of impending meals: all beefy gravy and over-boiled vegetables. With the ambience of light jazz piano muzak playing softly in the background, it was the perfect environment to watch the silhouettes of seagulls floating lazily over the horizon.

Inside the bar, Kitty watched a couple playing footsie beneath one table. They were like a pair of ducks in that they were calm, cool and composed above the surface of the table, yet beneath they were frantically paddling and pawing at one another. She guessed they were work colleagues who had decided to become closer whilst away on a business trip and that thought soured her good mood. Her smile faltered into a sneer because Kitty didn't like the idea of infidelity.

She was passionate about seagulls, herring gulls in particular, and believed they could illustrate an exemplary way of living. Seagulls usually mated for life and did not give in to cravings for infidelity. Seagulls were caring parents that shared the responsibility for incubating eggs and feeding young. Indeed, young seagulls were often found in nursery flocks, overseen by protective fathers. Seagulls, Kitty thought, could teach humans an awful lot about good behaviour. They certainly weren't weak vessels that allowed their sublimated urges to be made manifest beneath the table of a hotel bar, whilst they pretended to have a surface level of composure.

She turned away from the adulterous couple, allowing her sneer of disdain to spread more broadly before she fixed her gaze on the flamingo standing at the bar. Of course, the woman wasn't really a specimen from the *phoenicopterus ruber* family, but dressed in salmon pink, with a long slender figure and a long skinny neck, the resemblance was unmistakable. The woman's posture helped to sustain the image for Kitty because she was standing against the wall, with one leg raised so her knee pushed through the split of her short salmon pink skirt.

Flamingos were fatuous creatures, Kitty thought tiredly. They spent most of their time preening, sleeping, resting, or feeding and she thought the woman at the bar looked like someone who would have listed three of those four things as her primary hobbies. She was clearly skinny enough to look like she'd not had a good meal in the last month, but she also seemed to be extremely flamingo-vain, as evidenced by the way she kept admiring her reflection in the mirror.

"Seagull lady," cawed a small voice.

Kitty turned to see a dirty-faced child pointing at her whilst its blushing grandmother tried to wrestle it into obedience.

"Shush now, Archie," the grandmother insisted. "Don't be rude."

"Seagull lady! Seagull lady!" called the child.

"Shush now," insisted the grandmother. "And you know it's rude to point."

Kitty was going to tell the grandmother that pointing was the least rude thing about the child's behaviour, but the concierge chose that moment to appear behind the reception desk and, not for the first time since she had made his acquaintance, she thought he looked like a busy man with no time to spare on the niceties of a pleasant exchange.

"What do you want, Kitty?" the concierge asked. "This is teatime, and you know it's the busiest time of the day for me."

"Seagull lady," the child called again.

Kitty shot the little brat a scowl and then turned back to face the concierge. "It's the first of the month," Kitty explained. "You know what I want."

28

He was shaking his head. "Business is down this month. It has been for a couple of months and I'm thinking that the disappearances you've caused might be responsible. You can't expect me to meet exorbitant payments like the ones you demand when you're sabotaging my business."

"It's the first of the month," Kitty repeated. She glared at him with cold and unblinking eyes, acting as though he hadn't spoken. "You know what I want."

The concierge lowered his voice. "I lost two customers to your vicious birds last week," he whispered. "I'm sure you'll be grateful to hear that I did a lot of quick thinking and some industrial levels of covering up and lying to the police."

Kitty said nothing for a moment, simply studying him in silence. Before their measured glares could turn into a staring contest, she nodded sagely and said, "Clearly, you've done it right. Otherwise, you'd be in jail."

"That's not the point," he snapped.

"That's exactly the point," Kitty argued. "Clearly, you've done it right. Otherwise, you'd be under serious investigation. And someone would be asking about the shiny black sports car you're now driving when it's late at night and you think no one is watching you."

The concierge had the good grace to blush. "Something needed to be done with the sportscar," he mumbled. Seeing that her unblinking gaze continued to stare through him, he shook his head angrily, reached into the cash register at the reception desk and pulled out a sheaf of notes. "There's a grand there," he spluttered, pushing the money into Kitty's hands. "That's all I can afford this month, so you'll have to be satisfied with that."

Kitty took the money and began to count through the notes as he stood behind the reception desk shuffling from one foot to the other. "This isn't enough," she told him. "I needed two grand from you."

"That's all I can afford for your extortion fees."

"Extortion fees?" Kitty shook her head in reproof and said, "Extortion is a form of theft that occurs when the offender obtains money or property from someone using coercion. To constitute coercion, a threat of violence or destruction of property has to be committed." She studied him with an expression of innocent naivety and said, "Have I ever coerced you with threats of violence or destruction of property?"

"You've got those fucking seagulls," the concierge grumbled. "Those killer fucking seagulls."

"Killer seagulls?" Kitty laughed. "Are you suggesting I've trained seagulls so that they can do my bidding and attack on command?" Her false laughter was loud enough to ring from the walls of the hotel foyer. "Do you think anyone in their right mind would treat such an accusation with any credulity? Surely you realise that most people hearing that would think you were deluded?"

"I know it sounds deluded," the concierge agreed. He looked like a man struggling to say what he believed. The next words that came from his mouth seemed to have been spat from his lips with obvious reluctance. "But I know that you do have some control over those damned birds."

Kitty shrugged and put the money into the pocket of her coat.

"You flatter me as some sort of seagull snake charmer," she said easily. "And, whilst I'm sure it would be a blessing to have such an ability, I don't think that's something a modern court would ever be able to prove beyond reasonable doubt." She lifted her gaze to meet his and there was no mirth or amusement in her expression. "I need the other grand by tomorrow night," she insisted.

He started to reply, an excuse about why that was impossible, but she spoke over him before he could utter a syllable.

"Make sure it's paid in full," she told him. "If there's a shortfall, I worry there's a strong chance that your wife or your son might be attacked by one of my allegedly trained seagulls." She gave him a twisted smile and said, "And you know how sharp their bills can be, don't you?"

The concierge looked ready to bellow an outraged response, but Kitty didn't allow him the opportunity. She swirled the coat around her hips as she turned and marched from the hotel. The only thing that stopped it from being a flawless exit was the whiny child calling after her with the words, "Seagull lady! She's a seagull lady!"

"Yes, I am," Kitty thought bitterly. "And if any of my lovelies see you walking on the promenade today, I'm going to have them sweep down and take out both of your bratty little eyeballs."

All Things Fight and Beautiful

Deacon thought, when it came to the Punch and Jodie Show, there were some significant differences between the organised men's fights and the organised women's matches. The most obvious of these differences was, instead of taking place on the seafront, near an encroaching tide and beneath the stars, the women's fighting took place in the after-hours basement bar of a town centre pub called The Cock and Bull.

It was three in the morning. The air was still perfumed with lager, bitter, scotch and Lynx Africa. A space on the dance floor had been cleared and the two competitors were brought out to the cheers of a loud and boorish crowd.

"Ladies and gentlemen," Jodie called, taking centre stage and motioning for the audience to shut up and listen. Once again she was dressed all in black, like some aging Goth who hadn't found colour as she left her teenage years. She wasn't particularly tall or attractive. In truth, Deacon thought she kept her looks hidden beneath a baseball cap and an upturned collar. But she held the attention of the audience as if this was the halftime show at the Superbowl. "Welcome to tonight's girl-on-girl match of the Punch and Jodie Show," she declared.

The applause erupted again. This time there were a handful of whooping cheers as the enthusiasm reached a vocal climax. Deacon suspected it was the words 'girl-on-girl' that had prompted this reaction and he found himself sneering with contempt for all those watching. There was something contemptible about the salacious appetites of the male audience members at a girl-on-girl deathmatch and he couldn't conceal his sneer of disdain.

He supposed that one of the main differences between the men's fights and the women's fights was that the women in the fights always looked more human than their male equivalents. Deacon had always thought that the guys in a hobo fight looked like something less than human. They were all straggly hair, dirt, sweat, and scaly signs of skin disease that looked suspiciously like *dermatitis neglecta*. In contrast, the women looked like they had been freshly washed and bathed before battle commenced. Each had their hair worn up in a bun. Each looked as though every nook and cranny had been soaped, scrubbed, shaved and lovingly patted dry.

Of course, just like their male counterparts, the women did not look happy to be participating. Clearly neither of the female fighters was comfortable with the near-nudity and they both looked pained by the barbwire costumes that adorned their bodies. Whereas the men had simply had barbwire tied around their bandaged fists, the women were dressed in impractical barbwire bras, paired with matching barbwire panties, and long barbwire gloves. The outfits concealed nothing and seemed to make every movement sufficiently uncomfortable to inspire a flinch of distress. The barbs were clearly sharp because Deacon could see tears of blood dripping from Cheryl's breasts and from between her thighs.

The sight gave him a boner.

"In the red corner," Jodie declared, pointing at Cheryl, "we have Cheryl Ray Robinson." Cheryl stood there looking surly and defensive as a grumble of applause went around the room. She was clearly not a favourite for the punters, and that absence of confidence made her look small and vulnerable in the dimly lit venue. She shifted a feral glance from one face to another, looking as though she desperately wanted to escape and was anxious to find a way out. She was obviously frightened, not sure what was happening, and seeming a little puzzled by the nickname she'd been given. Deacon ducked behind a tall guy in the crowd before her gaze could fall on him.

"In the blue corner," Jodie continued, "a firm favourite amongst regulars here at the Punch and Jodie Show, we have the legendary killer griller: Georgina Foreman."

Georgina went to the centre of the ring and raised both hands to encourage more cheers from the crowd. Deacon glanced at her and realised the woman's name wasn't Georgina: this was just a stage-name Jodie had selected to make the fighting sound more authentic. He recognised Ellie from a handful of Blackpool clubs and her work as a former teacher. He didn't like to think how she'd ended up as one of Jodie's fighters and he was sure he wasn't ever going to ask her the question.

Ellie / Georgina was a formidable figure, tall and muscular, her bare skin scarred by lines from previous fights that had torn through flesh, muscle and tattoos. Looking closely, Deacon could see she'd lost a nipple at some point, and she also had a line of white scar tissue running from her forehead, through one split eyebrow, and down through her cheek. He suspected the blue eyepatch she wore was covering a multitude of horrors that would have been too distasteful to behold and he thanked the forces of propriety that had gone to the trouble of concealing those more unsightly injuries.

"You've got ten minutes to put on the last of your bets," Jodie told the crowd. "And then the deathmatch begins." She stepped off the dance floor and walked directly to Deacon. Nodding back at Cheryl she told him, "That's the shittiest excuse for a fighter I've seen in a long time."

Deacon shrugged. "You'll get a couple of rounds out of her," he said, not caring if that was true or not. "How much are you paying me for her?"

"You think she's worth payment?"

Deacon said nothing and waited for her to relent. There were ways to negotiate, and he knew that showing indignation in response to this comment would only make it difficult to agree a fair price.

Eventually, Jodie rolled her eyes and said, "Should we make it a bet?"

"What were you thinking?"

"If she wins you get two grand," Jodie told him. "If she loses, you pay me a grand, and you have to help my team dispose of the body."

Deacon scowled but nodded agreement. If he'd been at the basement bar with no knowledge of Cheryl, he wouldn't have placed a bet on her, even at Jodie's generous odds of 2 - 1. Jodie was putting on pressure to make him seem like he had confidence in Cheryl when Deacon figured the poor bitch would be dead meat before the first minute had elapsed. They shook on the bet and Deacon went to the bar to grab a beer whilst Jodie took more bets on the outcome of the fight.

He contemplated going to Cheryl and trying to chat with her but, since he was the one who had virtually sold her into slavery as a deathmatch participant, he doubted she would have any desire to talk. He briefly thought of taking her a porn star martini, Cheryl's cocktail of choice, but he figured she would only throw the drink in his face if he did make the gesture. He also doubted he would be able to get a drink past any of Jodie's diligent staff, who were monitoring the fighters and keeping unruly audience members at an arm's length. There were two guards on either side of each fighter and a further three mingling with the crowd like the security contingent at a presidential rally. Deacon thought it was a testament to Jodie's organisational skills that the events were run with such efficiency. He had never seen any drunks or crowd violence at a Punch and Jodie Show. He had never heard of any fight falling subject to a police enquiry. In fact, to the best of his knowledge, the local law enforcement was oblivious to the existence of the deathmatches. It impressed Deacon because, even though they were illegal, underground deathmatches: the administrative skill of Jodie and her team was flawless.

"All bets should now be placed," Jodie announced from the centre of the stage. "Barman," she called. "If you can give us a little ambient music and some appropriate mood lighting, I think we're ready to begin."

The barman gave a brief salute, turned to the control desk beside his till, and his fingers scurried over the buttons.

A roar of thrash metal erupted from the speakers.

The dim lights were instantly replaced by flashing reds and blues that beat in time to the music's rhythm. The lights were eerily reminiscent of parked police cars and Deacon thought that added to the tense atmosphere that was created. It was like waiting in a room for the inevitable arrest.

"Ladies," Jodie screamed into the microphone. "You're fighting to the death."

And then she was leaving the dance floor and Cheryl and Georgina stood alone in the centre of a pack of baying enthusiasts. Cries of "Kill the bitch," and, "Rip her tits off," shrieked from the audience. Whoops of eager support and yelled calls to action were screamed so they could be heard over the thrash metal.

Deacon sipped at his beer and watched intently.

Georgina rolled her broad shoulders back and flexed her biceps. She was a formidable figure and he understood why Cheryl took a faltering step away from her. Cheryl's gaze was flitting around the bar, looking for an escape route and repeatedly finding none. When Georgina took another step toward her, Deacon thought Cheryl was going to run. Instead, she threw herself at the taller woman and battered her sides with barbwire punches that landed heavily on her hips and kidneys.

The attack took Georgina by surprise. She tried swatting at Cheryl with her forearms, but her opponent was relentless. Cheryl kept punching and punching until she had opened a series of small tears above Georgina's hips and spatters of blood were flying across the faces of those in the front row of the audience.

"And the challenger is going in with full fury," Jodie called into the microphone. "Cheryl Ray Robinson is coming out hitting her opponent with relentless jabs. Georgina Foreman is trying to deflect her but she's no match for the ferocity of this fierce and unexpected assault."

Cheers and boos resounded from the audience. Some wag shouted, "Illegal move," and a couple of others chuckled at the idea of any move being illegal in an underground deathmatch.

Georgina slammed her knee into Cheryl's crotch and the rapid punches stopped. Georgina staggered backward, clearly needing a moment's respite, whilst Cheryl fell to her knees, her eyes squeezed together around tears of pain. Fresh blood was trickling from between her thighs and Deacon realised the knee to Cheryl's groin had driven one of the barbs from her barbwire panties into a place that was clearly very sensitive to such attacks.

He pressed his legs together, as though he could feel the discomfort that had clearly taken Cheryl to her knees. Deacon realised, in dismissing Cheryl as the loser before the battle had begun, he had underestimated Cheryl's ability to put up a good fight. The punches she had thrown were short, sharp and had clearly rocked the current titleholder. If not for the unfortunate knee to her lady bits, Deacon thought Cheryl might have had a chance of taking Georgina out in the first minute.

Then Georgina was back in the fight and delivering a kick to Cheryl's face that came close to taking her head off. The brutality was violent and relentless but Cheryl clearly wasn't going to be easily overthrown by such a response. Cheryl dragged her opponent to the floor and, within seconds, she was kneeling over Georgina and battering her face with blows from the barbwire gloves she wore.

Deacon saw Georgina's lip explode and her nose shatter. The woman was doing a good job of protecting herself in the circumstances, but it seemed no one in the after-hours bar had planned on Cheryl being quite so competitive. Georgina's eye patch was torn from her face revealing a dark hole where an eyeball had once sat. The flesh of her eyelid was flayed and Deacon thought it was like looking at something unfinished and alien.

Cheryl slammed a punch into Georgina's other eye.

Georgina howled.

Deacon thought he heard the squelch of a barb piercing the woman's eyeball. Of course, given the loudness of the music and the baying of the crowd, that seemed impossible. But he thought he heard the slick whisper of metal piercing skin, followed by the soft whistle of vitreous humour, eyeball-juice for want of a better term, squirting over Cheryl's knuckles.

Cheryl staggered away from Georgina.

Instead of pursuing her, Georgina lay on the floor with her hands over her eyes, screaming for assistance. "She blinded me," Georgina cried. "The bitch blinded me."

Deacon had never heard such anguish in a human cry.

"Finish her," Jodie told Cheryl.

"Fuck off," Cheryl said. She sounded breathless with exertion and self-loathing.

"It's a deathmatch," Jodie insisted. "To win, you need to kill your opponent."

Cheryl shrugged. "Then it looks like I've lost." She glanced down at her fists and seemed to realise that she was still wearing barbwire gloves whilst Jodie was only protected by a man's coat and a hat that covered her eyes. A gleam came into her eye that made Jodie step hurriedly back.

One of Jodie's assistants fired a taser.

The gun made a popping sound, followed by the sizzle of electricity as Cheryl dropped to her knees and then fell face first to the dancefloor. Jodie pulled a stubby handgun from inside her jacket and pointed it at Georgina's head.

Georgina was oblivious to her, still clutching at her useless eyes and sobbing, "She blinded me. The fucking bitch blinded me."

Jodie fired a single gunshot into Georgina's head and the entire room fell silent. The barman switched off the music and the baying crowd stopped chanting and calling immediately. The only noise now came from Cheryl who was whimpering on the floor as the taser's charge continued to shiver through her body.

"We have a new champion," Jodie told the crowd. "Those of you who'd bet on Cheryl Ray Robinson to win, you can collect your winnings on the way out. The rest of you can try and recoup your losses on the Bispham seafront next Wednesday night."

"Did you say I've got two grand coming to me for Cheryl's win?" Deacon asked eagerly.

Jodie rolled her eyes. "I'll have your two grand once you've finished helping my team dispose of that body," she said, pointing her gun at Georgina.

"Are you serious?"

"Does it look like I'm doing stand-up comedy?"

"Why do I have to help get rid of the body?"

"Because you want paying for the player you sold me," Jodie reminded him. "And, unless you do exactly as I say, you're not going to see a penny of that two grand you're after." She snapped her fingers at two of her operatives, a burly black guy and a butch-looking woman, and said, "Deacon's coming with you on the clean-up crew."

The Hunt for Fred October

Dave knew his target's name wasn't really Fred October even though that was what the initial message had said. A second email had come through from the client to say he was looking for *Fred Okeborne*, and the October surname had been a mistake put in by autocorrect. But Dave had grinned at the name 'Fred October', and he found himself using that epithet to go with the photograph he now had. The amusement of calling the client Fred October helped his mind balance the horror of what had happened to the poor bastard.

Fred October looked to be in his early 40s and his well-scrubbed features stared sullenly back at Dave from the blown-up passport photo that had been sent through. Not that Fred's features would be so well-scrubbed if the guy had been living rough for the past month, Dave thought. The chances were, there would be a substantial growth of beard on his cheeks, an oily layer of dirt and grime covering the rest of his face, and residual traces of the typical weathering that happened to a down-and-out living on the streets of a seaside town during the tail-end of the summer season. Dave knew that three nights of living rough could age a man more than a decade. An entire month, if it didn't kill him, would make the poor bugger look unrecognisable.

But still, he thought the photograph was a good place to start. That, and the fact that Fred had a finger missing from his right hand. Even if Fred's features had changed from when the photograph was taken, people often remembered something as distinctive as a missing finger.

"Fred October," Dave muttered, trying to distract the downward spiral of his nihilistic thoughts with the silliness of the misunderstood name. This time the misnomer didn't even raise a smile. But, he thought grimly, with this case, there wasn't a lot for him to smile about.

According to the client, Fred October had been a respectable figure in middle-management at a local supermarket in his hometown of Sheffield. Fred had been liked, trusted, married and the father to two children. From the outside it looked like he had everything a man could want. But, according to Fred's brother, it seemed he woke up one morning and no longer wanted any of those things he possessed. He only wanted to escape all of life's pressures. Instead of going into work he walked to the nearby train station of Meadowhall and bought a single to Blackpool. He'd taken no change of clothes, no phone, no bank card and no more money than was in his back pocket.

This was the part that Dave found so horrifying.

He felt sickened at the notion that someone could wake up one morning and decide their life had no meaning or value. It was even worse to realise that Fred October had come to the conclusion that his existence would be better served by being an unemployed hobo in a town more than a hundred miles away from his workplace, his family and his home. The idea that so much of what a person had built for himself could be so easily discarded, filled Dave with a queasy sense of despair because, if it could happen to someone as normal looking as Fred October, it could happen to anyone.

Dave wondered if he could ever be in Fred's horrific situation.

The brother had said that Fred occasionally drank too much, took antidepressants and carried a lot of stress from his work. Dave thought that sounded so similar to his own situation that he and Fred could have been twin spirits. The brother claimed Fred had some financial troubles, but he admitted it was nothing more than the average debt incurred by anyone living paycheque to paycheque. To Dave's mind, none of Fred's issues seemed sufficient to make someone run away from work, home and family, and resume their existence on the lowest rung of capitalism's ladder. In truth, according to what he'd heard from the brother, Fred's lifestyle, with family a home and job security, seemed much better than the miserable day-to-day that Dave was currently living.

He wondered if such impulses were restricted to the overworked, the cash-strapped and the chemically controlled Fred's of this world: or if such reactions could be squeezed out of anyone if they were struck by the same unfortunate barrage of circumstances and a flatlined mood. If the latter was possible, then the notion that anyone could become another Fred October was the most disturbing thing

Dave could imagine. He shivered at the thought of waking up one morning and following the example set by Fred October: a sullen walk to the train station, a brief journey to a new life, and then a hollow existence as one of society's unseen pariahs.

Dave's own work as a self-employed private investigator was not the most lucrative or prestigious position. Dave now fretted that he was no more than two bounced cheques away from following Fred's example and going to live with the hobos in a world where responsibilities no longer mattered, and the only ambition was to get enough money for a bottle of something cheap and 40% proof. The idea of facing such a bleak future made his bowels clench with unease and he quietly vowed to himself that he was going to solve this case as a priority before any other consideration that landed on his desk. It was the same sort of superstitious impulse that would have him throwing balled up sticky-notes at the bin in his office, and telling himself that hitting three in a row would guarantee success. It sounded like a ridiculous superstition, but he believed, only by solving this case, locating Fred October and potentially delivering the guy back to the welcoming arms of his family home, could Dave avoid suffering a similar fate.

His investigation had taken him to a couple of local hostels and Dave learned that Fred had been seen at one of the locations two weeks earlier. It was easy to make an ID on the man because, aside from having a copy of the client's photograph on his phone, the missing finger on Fred's right hand had made him memorable. Dave had shown the photograph to hostel staff who shrugged and shook their heads. However, when Dave asked where they thought 'Freddie Four-Fingers' could now be found, they acknowledged that he had been there. Admittedly, most of them shrugged sympathetically and explained that they didn't have the resources to keep track of every service-user they processed. But, because they remembered Freddie Four-Fingers, they did tell Dave that Jimmy the Limp had been seen chatting with Fred and they figured, if he could track down Jimmy the Limp, Dave would be one step closer to finding Fred October.

That lead had taken Dave to the town centre.

Late at night, Blackpool was renowned for drunken excess, ribaldry, and potential violence. Those hobos that hadn't found a room in a hostel for the night were usually panhandling outside pubs and nightclubs, bumming cigarettes, spare change and sympathy drinks. This was where Dave had been told he would find Jimmy the Limp and he kept scouring the streets, looking for the vaguely familiar figure of one of the town's most recognisable tramps.

He took a trip along Abingdon Street and then cut down Clifton Street toward the promenade where he could see a small crowd had gathered outside one of the seafront bars. A chill wind blew in from the Irish Sea but, because the day had been balmy, the movement of air was pleasant. It salted the breeze and pressed beads of welcome cool moisture to sweaty brows. Dave scanned the crowd outside the pub and then turned his gaze toward the seafront.

Bingo!

Jimmy the Limp, a tall tramp who invariably wore a dirty red baseball cap and moved with a distinctly uneven gait, was standing outside the entrance to the North Pier. He looked to be engaged in a chat with a professional do-gooder: a man wearing chinos, a sweater, and a tweed sports jacket. The do-gooder looked like he had just stepped from a university degree and was filled with bright ideas for how to eradicate the problems of the homeless. As Dave got closer, he realised it was worse than a university degree in do-gooding: the guy was holding flyers that mentioned Jesus.

"A fucking God-botherer," Dave thought in despair. He rolled his eyes and hurried over as he called for Jimmy's attention. "Jimmy? Jimmy the Limp?" Dave yelled. "Is that you?"

Jimmy gave him a questioning glance. The professional do-gooder frowned with disapproval. He clutched protectively at his sheaf of flyers.

"What you want?" Jimmy asked.

Dave stepped closer and held up his mobile, showing the photograph of Fred October. "Do you recognise this guy? He's called Freddie Four-Fingers."

Jimmy squinted at the image for a moment and then studied Dave carefully. "What's in it for me if I've seen him?"

Dave produced a tenner and pointed it in Jimmy's face. "Where will I find him?"

"You shouldn't be giving money to the homeless," the do-gooder told Dave. "If you give him that money, he's going to spend it on drugs or alcohol."

Dave gave the do-gooder a withering glare and shrugged. "That's all I was going to do with it, so I don't see the problem." He turned back to Jimmy and said, "Do you know where I'd find this guy?"

Jimmy the Limp nodded and snatched the tenner from Dave's hand. "Sally Army. South Shore." The ten pound note had disappeared into Jimmy's pocket before he said, "You going to hurt him?"

The do-gooder was also staring at Dave, as though anxious to hear the response to that question.

It was not a question that Dave had been expecting so he shook his head, wondering why anyone would think he wanted to hurt a member of the homeless community. "His family are concerned for him," Dave explained. "I'm just going to make sure he's OK and let him know that his loved ones are worried about him."

"I talked with him," Jimmy said solemnly. "Freddie came here because he wanted to get away from those loved ones."

Dave nodded. "And, if the wants of Freddie Four-Fingers paid my bills, I wouldn't trouble him. But I've got a client that's paying good money for an update on his whereabouts and wellbeing."

The do-gooder snorted with disdain. "You're not helping here, are you?" he snapped. "You're hounding innocent men just so you can line your own pockets. Do you think that's a good thing?"

Dave shrugged again. "One of us two has given Jimmy the Limp a tenner this evening. The other has just tried to bore his tits off with talk about social work and some flyer telling him how Jesus wants to help. When Jimmy finally finds somewhere to lay his head tonight, which one of us do you think will have better contributed to his good night's sleep?"

"That's a tad reductive, don't you think?"

Dave ignored the do-gooder. He was tempted to give Jimmy the Limp a second tenner, just to annoy the God-botherer. The only thing that stopped him was the knowledge that it might be difficult to claim back so much in unreceipted expenses for information he'd gleaned from a single contact.

"Sally Army, South Shore," Dave repeated.

Jimmy nodded.

Dave glanced at the do-gooder and then told Jimmy, "If it turns out that Jesus loves you, tell him no tongues on a first date." Without waiting to see how his comment had been received, Dave took a taxi down to South Shore, got a receipt for his expenses, and walked cautiously to the doorway of the Salvation Army hostel. It wasn't the worst part of the town but, after eleven o'clock at night, it was dark, lit only by a faltering streetlamp, and the figures that lurked in the shadows made Dave's bowels tingle with apprehension. There was a tramp standing guard on the door, a smouldering roll-up clutched between his dirt-stained fingertips. He wore a tattered coat, fingerless gloves and a beanie pulled low over his ears. Seeing Dave approach the door, he held out a hand and asked, "Got any spare change?"

"Fuck off," Dave grunted.

"Thank you anyway," the tramp said, raising the hand he had been holding and touching his brow as a sign of deference.

Dave pulled the phone from his pocket and opened it to show the photograph of Fred October. "Have you seen this guy?"

The tramp licked his lips and wiped his nose with the back of his hand. "I reckon I might know someone who looks like that. Is he called Freddie?"

Dave felt a moment of self-loathing. His first response to this man had been to tell him to fuck off. He had treated him as though he was less than human and not deserving the simple courtesy of a polite response. And yet the man was still acting pleasantly toward Dave and potentially offering a lead. The idea that anyone's life could be reduced to these levels of humiliating misery made his stomach tighten with unease.

He pulled a tenner from his back pocket and pointed it in the tramp's face. "Is he in there?" he asked, nodding at the hostel.

"He was last night," the tramp admitted. "But not tonight. Tonight he's up in Bispham. They say he's involved with the Punch and Jodie Show."

Dave didn't hear the final four words because his mobile chose that moment to ring. He pushed the tenner at the tramp who accepted it gratefully. After pulling his phone from his pocket, Dave glanced at the Caller-ID and saw it was a call from one of the insurance companies he had previously worked with. Knowing that insurance companies paid stupid money for minimal services, he turned away from the tramp and answered the call. "Who's this?"

"Dave?"

Dave recognised Lloyd's voice straight away. "What can I do for you?" Dave asked.

"Do you know of the Cleveleys Hotel, just outside Blackpool?"

Dave considered the question for a moment. "It's a ten minute drive from where I'm currently standing," he admitted. "Why do you ask?"

"One of the car dealerships that I work with has had a Pagani Roadster go missing. The guy who was leasing it has gone AWOL for the past fortnight. The car is nowhere to be seen but we've got a GPS tracker on it that says it's sauntering around the Blackpool area and parking at a garage owned by the Cleveleys Hotel. Are you able to pick it up?"

Dave hesitated, remembering the personal vow he had made earlier. He wanted to solve the case of Fred October to banish the superstitious notion that he too could succumb to the same fate as Freddie Four-Fingers. It was important that he pursue every lead, including this tramp's gibberish about the man being in Bispham at a Punch and Judy show. But he also knew, it didn't do to give anything less than immediate service to people with pockets as deep as Lloyd's.

"What's a Pagani Roadster?"

"It's a supercar," Lloyd explained. "And this car is not cheap. There's thirty grand for you if you can retrieve it for us."

Dave's decision was made instantly. "Send me the GPS info, and I'll have it for you within twenty-four hours." Dave's promise to the gods that linked his fortunes with Fred October were suddenly forgotten as he said, "For thirty grand, I'll have it back to you before the day's gone."

He ended the call and looked around for the tramp who had been telling him where to find Fred, intending to pick up on that investigation as soon as he'd retrieved the Pagani Roadster. The door to the hostel was closed, the street was empty, and Dave was alone with no idea of how he could find Fred October save for some reference to the Punch and Jodie show: and he hoped to Christ that sort of barbarity hadn't started up again.

Beach Body Ready

Deacon sat in the middle seat of the Transit. The driver, on his right, was a burly black guy who everyone called Big Charlie. He wore a tan survival jacket with zippers, pockets and padding that only added to his bulk. He didn't talk much and, because of the man's size and reputation for being a hard-ass, Deacon made no attempt to break the silence that surrounded him.

Big Charlie's colleague, Annabelle, sat on Deacon's left and she was equally unapproachable. Annabelle's hair was shorn at the sides and her fringe was greased into a rockabilly quiff. Even without the combat jacket, the military boots and the roll-up cigarette hanging from the corner of her mouth, Deacon would have tagged her as a lesbian. Because she was dressed like an extra from *Orange is the New Black*, he figured identifying her sexuality was a no-brainer, which meant he had no reason to talk with her either. What was the point of a straight guy talking to a gay woman? He wasn't even sure they spoke the same language.

Staring directly out of the windscreen, trying to make it seem like the question was directed at either or neither of his travelling companions, Deacon asked, "Where are we taking her?"

"We're burying her," Annabelle told him.

Deacon resisted the urge to roll his eyes. Burying would mean manual labour. The chances were good that Jodie had sent him along with these two to do some heavy lifting. He shook his head and wondered if there were easier ways to make illegal money.

"Where are we burying her?"

"The usual location," Big Charlie grunted.

Deacon ground his teeth together and tried not to show his frustration. This was his first time travelling with Jodie's hired muscle and he had no idea where bodies were usually buried. He figured the location was secure, because he'd never heard of anyone finding one of the brutalised hobo corpses. But that didn't mean he had any idea as to where the location might be.

"How long is this going to take?"

"You ask a lot of questions," Annabelle observed.

"I'd ask a lot less if I got some straight answers."

Big Charlie slammed on the brakes. Deacon felt his stomach lurch and he wondered if his confrontational tone had been a mistake. To his relief Annabelle pulled open her door and disappeared into the night. Once his heartbeat had stopped hammering, Deacon realised that Big Charlie had been intending to slam on the brakes at this point and he hadn't stopped the van because of anything that had been said. Deacon drew a deep breath that sounded like a sigh of relief and asked, "Is this where we're burying her?"

Big Charlie shook his head. "Annabelle's just here to get the Cat," he explained.

Deacon said nothing. He had no idea why Annabelle needed a cat, and he had no intention of asking Big Charlie for clarification. The guy was trying to be deliberately ambiguous, and Deacon did not want to give him the satisfaction of knowing that he was puzzled. He considered going for the hip flask of scotch he kept in his breast pocket but decided it would be more prudent to stay sober and clear-minded in case he needed to have sharp wits for anything that was about to happen.

Annabelle climbed into the transit.

Deacon glanced at her and said, "Where's your cat?"

She frowned, looking at him as though he was stupid. "It's hooked to the back of the van."

Deacon glanced toward the wing-mirror on her side and saw that she had attached a short trailer to the towbar of the transit. The trailer held a 7T Caterpillar digger and Deacon understood this was the Cat that Big Charlie had mentioned. The van pulled away from the kerb, dragging its cargo behind it and, within a few minutes, they were on the promenade and headed out of Blackpool through the suburb of Anchorsholme. Big Charlie drove across the tram tracks and then took a sloping incline that led down to the beach.

He killed the headlights and it was suddenly pitch black. The roar of the sea was faraway and Deacon felt as though he was standing at the end of the world. The idea that he was out in such an isolated spot with two criminals and a corpse was enough to make his bowels twist. Yes, he'd attended hobo deathmatches. Yes, he'd given Cheryl over to become one of the slave participants in such barbarity. But this was a danger that could easily threaten his own safety. Goosebumps prickled down his spine and along his forearms.

"We're close enough," Annabelle decided.

Big Charlie eased on the brake and drew them to a halt. They looked to be about ten yards away from the edge of the sea. Typically, the tide on this part of the coastline was either pressed tight against the concrete sea defences, and splashing over onto the walkways that ran parallel to the seafront, or it was so far out visitors needed a Transit like Big Charlie's to get close to the water's edge.

"This is where we're burying her?" Deacon tried not to sound incredulous but it was difficult. Laying the body to rest on the sand seemed like a perfect way to expose everything they'd done. The chances of the corpse simply floating toward the shore, and being discovered by authorities, were dangerously high. Deacon thought, if that was what they were expected to do, he might as well write out a confession now and tape it to the woman's body. "You're just going to dump her in the sea?" he marvelled.

"No," Annabelle said simply. "We're not just dumping her in the sea. That's why I brought the Cat."

She climbed out of the Transit, walked to the back of the vehicle, and then drove the Cat from its trailer. It was a diesel engine designed to be used on a building site and it roared like a freshly released kraken. In the stillness of the night Deacon felt as though the three of them were now wearing a neon sign that demanded authorities come and look at them as they tried to covertly dispose of a body beneath the moonlight.

His eyes were growing used to the moonlit night when he saw Annabelle use the digger to scoop a big slice of wet sand from the seashore. Understanding swept over him and he realised Annabelle was digging a grave in the sand for the body.

"Is this safe?" he asked Big Charlie.

"None of them have come up to the surface yet," Big Charlie said simply. "And we've been doing this a while now." Silence stretched between them as Deacon stared out of the window and watched Annabelle manoeuvre the Cat, so it was digging a deeper trough into the sand. "We get as close to the edge of the outgoing tide as we dare," Big Charlie explained.

Given the guy's burly build and constant scowl, Deacon hadn't expected him to sound so intelligent.

"I've studied marine biology," Big Charlie added. "At this distance from the sea defences the displacement of the sand is minimal from the oncoming tides. Dropping something down six foot here means it's going to stay beneath the sand and never be seen again."

"You're kidding," Deacon marvelled.

Big Charlie shook his head. "Annabelle can get that digger down six or seven feet, then we drop in the body and cover it with sand. The tide is going to cover her resting place 90% of the time and, for that other 10%, the sea will have flattened the sand so that no one knows what secrets are hidden there."

Deacon stared at him in slack-jawed wonder. As far as ways of hiding bodies went, this had to be the most sophisticated method he could have imagined. The sea was going to hide the secret forever. The body was going to rot over time and the creatures that lived in the wet sand were going to destroy any lingering evidence.

"Is this all Jodie's idea?"

"She's got a brain on her," Big Charlie acknowledged. "She had the idea, sounded it off against Annabelle and me because she knew we both had degrees in marine biology. And we've been working with her ever since."

Deacon was shaking his head with admiration.

Big Charlie reached into the glove compartment and retrieved a bowie knife and a handheld paddle labelled 'security scanner.' "These are for you," Big Charlie said, handing them over.

Deacon recognised the security scanner as standard kit for nightclub doormen. It was a metal detector that would shriek if it picked up something dangerous like a knife or a length of pipe. Reluctantly, he took the paddle and the knife and asked, "What do I need these for?"

"My job is to drive us down here," Big Charlie explained. "I've got the Transit. I drive the Transit."

"Agreed," Deacon said.

"Annabelle digs the hole," Big Charlie went on. "She drives the Cat and knows how to use the scoopy-thing."

Hearing the word 'scoopy-thing', Deacon's faith in Big Charlie's credentials as a marine biologist began to flounder. He might know a lot about sand displacement and tidal motions but would it have taken much more for the man to learn a more sophisticated word than 'scoopy-thing'? He nodded his understanding, urging Big Charlie to get to the point.

"The body's going to be fairly safe once it's in Annabelle's hole, but there's always a danger that some prick with a metal detector might saunter along the seafront and accidentally locate what we've dropped there."

Now it was Deacon's turn to look puzzled. "How could a metal detector locate her?"

Big Charlie shrugged. "Necklace?" he guessed. "Earrings. Pussy piercing. Jewellery. Dental fillings. Any or all of the above." He reached for a carrier bag from the side of his seat and handed it to Deacon. "Anything you cut off her can be put in there and we'll dispose of it when we've done with the burial."

Understanding swept over Deacon with sickening clarity. For the first time that evening, he dearly wished he had just been there as muscle that was meant to lift and carry their unfortunate cargo. "Isn't it going to get messy in the back of the van?" he asked nervously.

Big Charlie shook his head. "Take her out on the sand. That way you won't leave any evidence in my van and the sea will get a chance to wash away any blood or mess that gets left behind."

Deacon's stomach tightened and he realised he was already on the verge of throwing up. Nodding grimly to himself, taking the paddle and the knife, he stepped out of the van and walked to the back of the vehicle so he could begin this distasteful chore.

The Early Bird

Councillor Andy Crawford stopped and glared at the abomination. It was barely eight in the morning. Sunlight had started to bleach the night from the sky over the sea. Andy's walk to work took him along the promenade past the Central Pier and, as he was glancing toward the horizon, he saw the abomination: a massive flock of seagulls all congregating around one dippy old pensioner sitting on a seafront bench whilst she tossed the contents from a bag of breadcrumbs at them. The bastard things were likely whitewashing the promenade around that bench with gallons of their putrid seagull shite, he thought. Andy was still annoyed that his colleagues in charge of health and safety legislation wouldn't allow him to poison the creatures because of some protection they had under the Wildlife and Countryside Act (1981). To his mind seagulls were disgusting vermin that spread filth and disease and needed eradicating. In Andy's opinion there was only one thing worse than seagulls.

"Kitty-bloody-Wakes," he muttered.

Outrage flooded through him, turning his cheeks purple and making his heartbeat race. To Andy it looked like there were a hundred or more birds with others falling from the dawn sky to join the seafront crowd. The majority were adults with brilliant white plumage fading to grey across their wings. There were also a handful of biscuit-coloured youngsters amongst the flock, screeching like vicious psychopaths and ready to kill for a morsel of food. Their shrill screams were so pained, if he hadn't seen what was happening, Andy would have thought he was hearing the aftermath of a brutal and violent murder.

"What the hell do you think you're doing?" Andy demanded as he strode over to the woman. A couple of the birds flapped away from him, but the majority remained undeterred by his approach. One or two of their heads turned to glare soullessly at him, cawing with obvious disdain. Andy tried to pay them no heed, but it was unnerving to be fixed by their haughty inhuman glares.

"Haven't you seen the instructions?" Andy demanded of the old woman. He pointed at a sign that had been tied to the set of railings that separated the promenade from the beach. The sign was a cheaply printed piece of yellow A4 paper that had been laminated for durability. The words on it were harsh and unambiguous. Written in bold black capitals on a canary yellow background they seemed to shout their message: DO NOT FEED THE SEAGULLS.

Behind him, a tram trundled swiftly past.

Normally the promenade transportation was loud enough to shake underfoot and make him need to raise his voice to be heard. With the squawk of so many outraged seagulls, Andy barely heard the vehicle.

"What's wrong with you?" he demanded of Kitty Wakes. "Are you an idiot?"

The woman looked up.

"Shit," he thought miserably. He took a step back, unnerved by the glint he had seen in her eye. He had known it was Kitty Wakes, the mad seagull woman from South Shore, but being this close to her was more disconcerting than he had anticipated. Andy didn't claim to know everyone in the town. His social circle was small and, being a widower and committed to his work at the council offices, he had little time or scope for friends and acquaintances. But he knew a handful of Blackpool's more eccentric personalities and Kitty Wakes from South Shore was one of those distinctive characters. Staring into her blank emotionless eyes, eyes that were not so dissimilar from the eyes staring at him from the flock of greedy, soulless birds at her feet, he wondered if she was potentially dangerous. There was almost certainly some risk of infection from the dirty old bag. Andy doubted she'd had a wash during this century, and she stank like restaurant waste at the height of a hot summer's day. But he also feared she might be dangerous because, judging from the soulless expression in her blank eyes, she was clearly nuttier than monkey shit.

"You shouldn't be feeding the seagulls," Andy said firmly. He pointed at the sign and said, "You know you shouldn't be doing that. We've put signs up."

Kitty sniffed. "I'm not feeding seagulls," she explained. "Seagulls don't exist."

Andy clenched his hands into fists and then unclenched them immediately. It would look bad if he was seen making threatening gestures toward a smelly, mental pensioner. And, thanks to the pedantry of some ornithological acquaintances on the council, he was familiar with the literalism behind her argument. Technically 'seagull' was not a classification of seabird. Instead, it was the layman's term that described a range of birds from the *Laridae* family, a genus that included more than fifty distinct species. The commonest type in Blackpool were the European herring gull, *Larus argentatus*. But, even if he listed every type of visiting gull from the commonest to the rarest, Andy knew he would not encounter the word 'seagull' in any official paperwork. However, Andy personally used the word 'seagull' because he also knew, if someone was writing a letter of complaint to him about the amount of seagull shit deposited on their business frontage, the letter writer wouldn't be pacified by the assurance that it wasn't seagull shit: it was most probably a guano specimen from *Larus argentatus*.

"You've seen the signage, Kitty," Andy continued. He was trying to quell his outrage, not wanting to be caught shouting at a pensioner but determined that she wouldn't get away with flouting the rules so blatantly. "You know we try and dissuade these dirty buggers from gathering because they present a health hazard. And this isn't the first time-"

He stopped abruptly as a seagull flapped dangerously close to his face. The flash of feathers scratched against his cheek and he raised a hand to try and protect himself.

"They don't like being called dirty buggers," Kitty said absently.

In that moment he hated her. The birds were flapping around his head, shrieking and cawing. He was close to panicking as the feathery fuckers inched nearer to his face with their beaks and wings. And Kitty Wakes was sitting placidly on the bench, chastising him in her softly spoken voice whilst occasionally throwing a handful of breadcrumbs for her flock to scavenge.

"You don't want to test me, Kitty," he said with low menace in his voice. He wasn't sure she could hear him clearly over the noise of the seagulls, but he could sense her stiffening and figured that most of his message was getting through. "You live in a council property," Andy reminded her. "Your heating is subsidised because of the council's social care benefits. If the council stops helping you, you're going to end up in an invidious situation."

"Are you threatening me, Councillor Crawford?" Kitty asked softly.

"I'm not threatening you," Andy said carefully. "I'm just reminding you that the council does a lot for you. And I don't want you suffering needlessly because a member of my team misinterprets your actions, and your disregard for my rules, as blatant ingratitude."

Kitty finally stood up from her bench. She was draped in the white coat with the grey sleeves that he had seen her wearing on a dozen previous occasions. It was the outfit that made her look like the seagull lady. Most of the flock remained at her feet, pecking at morsels of bread and tucking their wings neatly behind their backs. Two birds flew to her narrow shoulders and rested there patiently. Their inhuman eyes studied Crawford with expressions of cold contempt.

"Blatant ingratitude, Councillor Crawford?" Kitty echoed. "Is that how my actions might be interpreted?" She took a step toward him and one of the younger gulls broke from the flock on the ground and flapped angrily in Andy's face.

To his credit, Andy didn't flinch from the creature. Even though he was close enough to see the hook-like shape of the beak, and know it was mere inches from his eyes, he managed to remain poised and unmoved by the threat that the creature presented.

"Surely you know I can't be ungrateful for all you and the council have done for me?" she asked with sickening sweetness. "And the reason I can't be ungrateful is because you've done nothing."

"You're living in social housing-" Andy started.

He didn't get to finish the sentence. Three of the young gulls, speckled with brown and beige feathers on their adolescent bodies, took to the air and flew at him. They were screaming angrily, their cries so loud he wanted to fall to his knees and cover his ears for protection. He put up his arms to shield his face and felt something hard, sharp and merciless nip at the back of his hand. The pain was like being stabbed by a nail. Andy staggered back in surprise and felt another beak nip sharply at the upper lobe of his ear.

"Fuck!" Andy wailed.

"It took you years to put me in social housing," Kitty told him. "Decades if I remember rightly."

Andy was keeping his eyes clenched tightly shut whilst he batted at the air trying to repel the birds that were swooping down and pecking at him. He didn't dare open his mouth for fear that one of his attackers would grab at his lips or his tongue and tear at the soft flesh with its cruel beak.

"Once you'd put me in social housing," Kitty went on, "you made it impossible for my partner to move in with me."

Andy was shaking his head and batting blindly at the air around him. There were no longer three adolescent gulls attacking him. A dozen of the flock was flying at his face, head and throat and tearing chunks of skin away from him with unrelenting cruelty. He wanted to tell her that he hadn't made it difficult for Kitty to shack up with her partner: he was just implementing the rules that were in place for everyone. But he didn't have the opportunity to make his point. The birds that circled and tormented him were loud, territorial and terrifying.

"And," Kitty continued. "When I contacted you to say that something had happened to my partner, you didn't want to hear from me."

Andy flapped his hands above his head and got the satisfaction of striking something soft, light and feathery. In amongst the screams of the attacking birds he heard one of them squawk with displeasure at the rude assault and he wanted to grin as though he had accomplished something. His pleasure was short-lived because, as soon as he had struck the seagull, a beak caught his little finger and a flare of unbearable pain burned through his hand.

"You didn't want to hear from me, did you?" Kitty demanded.

"Missing people aren't something the council deals with," Andy spat. "Now, will you please get these flying rats away from me?"

Kitty snorted with disdain, clearly unhappy with the term 'flying rats'. "No," she agreed. "Just like everything else in my life: it's nothing to do with the council. My missing bloke is nothing to do with you. My home and heating are nothing to do with you. And, by extension, I think that how I go about getting him back is nothing to do with you."

Andy had stopped listening.

His eyes were squeezed tightly shut but, from the bloody shadows of dark and light, he could discern movement through his eyelids. Andy saw Kitty wave an arm in his direction. It looked like she was pointing at him and he heard the fluttering paper rustle of a thousand wings stiffening and lifting into the air. He dared to open his eyes for an instant, just to see what was happening.

That was when he saw Kitty was pointing at him with an accusatory finger. She had one arm outstretched and her mouth was open in a wide yawn of fury. In her other hand he saw she was holding a small silver trinket that looked to be shaped like a seagull. He tried listening to the noise she was making. He couldn't be sure, because the screech from the flock around her was so loud, but he thought she was making calls similar to those of the screaming seagulls she had been feeding. To make matters worse, her army of seagulls had risen behind her and they were determinedly flapping in the sky to keep themselves aloft. A myriad glittering eyes glared down at Andy with the menacing leer of predators about to attack.

Andy turned and ran.

He pulled his jacket over his head, protecting his face from those razor-tipped bills as he hurried blindly away from the gulls. He felt beaks and wings clawing at his face and hands. He twisted his head sharply in order to save himself and was only distantly aware of the seagull shit splashing down on his hunched back and slapping over his cowering shoulders. There was a moment when he thought he was going to lose his footing. He stumbled, almost went face first onto the tramlines but just managed to recover his balance at the last possible moment. He was determined to outrun the seagulls before they could do any serious damage to him and he figured he would be able to escape with nothing more than a few scratches to his hands and cheeks and a dry cleaner's bill for the damage done to his sport's jacket.

He was still thinking those thoughts when he stumbled into the path of a southbound tram. The impact killed him instantly.

The Repossession of Pagani Huayra

Sunlight was a few moments away from brightening the quiet streets behind the Cleveleys Hotel, meaning the world was caught in the gloaming haze of pre-dawn light. The shadows were long and dark. The world was holding its breath before beginning another day. Dave stared at the locked garage before him and waited until his taxi had driven away before he stepped closer to the unassuming building.

He had followed the GPS coordinates to a locked garage behind the Cleveleys Hotel. From what he'd been able to learn using Google on his taxi drive from South Shore to Cleveleys, the Pagani Huayra Roadster was either a supercar or a hypercar, or maybe the lovechild of both given its £3,000,000 price ticket.

The price had surprised him. He'd checked on three different websites and found the price listed at £2,600,000 on the cheapest one and £4,000,000 at the upper end of the price range. He'd thought the first one was a typo but, the more he read about the overpriced cars, the more he began to realise they cost millions of pounds and that explained why the job of retrieving this vehicle was so potentially lucrative.

Whilst conducting his research he'd watched an old clip from *Top Gear* on YouTube where Jeremy Clarkson had all but jizzed in his pants at the excitement of driving a Pagani Zonda R – one of the cousins to this particular motor. Clarkson made it sound like the pleasure of driving the car was slightly more satisfying than an orgasm and Dave had felt a little bit dirty after watching the video, as though he'd been voyeuristically admiring a middle-aged man indulging himself in a very private act. On reflection, he supposed that was exactly what he'd been watching.

Once the taxi was out of sight, Dave called Lloyd to tell him that the GPS coordinates led to a locked garage. He was staring at the low, flat-roofed building with its shuttered roller-door padlocked closed. The possibility of breaking into the garage did not seem beyond his abilities but he shrank from the idea of boldly marching up to the garage door and bursting inside.

"Is it in there?" Lloyd asked.

Dave shrugged. "The garage looks like it's locked," he explained. "And there's no window. If the GPS information is correct, it's in there. But I've got no way of confirming without taking some positive action."

"Can you break in and see if it's the Pagani?"

"I can break in," Dave admitted. "But if there are any alarms in place, and I suspect someone will have stuck alarms on a garage that holds a Pagani, I'm likely to trip all of them."

"Do it anyway," Lloyd decided. He seemed to have no problems making the decision for Dave's fate. "Despite its high price, hotwiring that thing shouldn't be a problem for someone with your skills. If the car's in there, I want you to retrieve it and drive it down to our Manchester offices. I'll text you the GPS details for the location."

"And if I get arrested?" Dave asked. "Or if the guy who owns the garage catches me and decides to batter the shit out of me? What happens in those circumstances?"

"Then you'll have earned the thirty grand fee you're getting for this operation," Lloyd assured him. "Now, get the car and let me know when it's safely parked at my garage in Manchester."

The call ended and Dave was left in the invidious situation of knowing that he had to perform a robbery to get the generous payday that Lloyd had offered. It was not a moral dilemma that troubled him for a great length of time. Technically, it was repossession rather than robbery. Admittedly, he would have to compromise a lock or two, but those crimes, compared to the taking of a car worth £3,000,000, were not comparable. Reminding himself that there was no other option if he wanted to see the money, Dave went to the garage door and studied the padlock.

It looked like the sort of combination lock he'd seen every morning in the gym, securing a cheap locker that held some sweaty muscle-head's wallet and car keys. He squatted down to the floor and played with the numbered dials for a couple of minutes before it popped open in his hands. Dave held himself still, fairly sure that no alarms had been triggered, but listening intently in case there was a distinctive sound telling him that he'd alerted the garage's owner.

Nothing.

After a few moments, he wondered if his worries about an advanced alarm system were seriously misplaced. The morning remained still and silent. Aside from the faraway whisper of the sea, and the distant screech of gulls, there was nothing to be heard. Slowly, trying to minimise the sound that was being made, Dave rolled the shutter up and peered into the garage.

There was an unusual smell and he wrinkled his nose in disgust as the stench hit the back of his nostrils. He turned on the light on his mobile phone and found himself staring at the beautiful sleek lines of the Pagani Huayra Roadster. It was an oily black colour that reflected every glint from his phone's torch. The car was stupidly low and ridiculously attractive, and Dave found himself grinning at the idea that he would have a chance to drive something so foolishly desirable.

And then he saw the body.

The man had once been dressed in a black waistcoat over a stiff white shirt, with a badge labelled 'concierge' over his right breast. Now the black waistcoat was powdered grey with dust and spattered white with bird shit. The white shirt was grimy with dirt and speckled with dried droplets of blood.

"Jesus," Dave grunted.

He placed a hand over his mouth to stop himself from retching, but it was a close call. The bubbling rush of his stomach contents yearned to burst through his throat at the obscenity before him and he had to dry swallow several times to stop the nausea rushing through his mouth.

The concierge no longer had any eyes. The sightless sockets stared at Dave as though they were beseeching him for some help. Holes had been made in his throat and, at first, Dave was not sure what could have caused such horrific damage to someone. Then he saw that the concierge was holding the corpse of a seagull and he guessed this had been a fight to the death between the man and a bird.

Dave stumbled back, still trying to keep his stomach contents down.

The seagull's neck had been snapped and the bird's corpse lolled in the concierge's hands. There was blood on its beak and the stains of the concierge's crimson handprint on its white breast.

"How the fuck does something like this happen?" he muttered. On top of that thought came the more pressing question: what was he meant to do now?

It was, he supposed, a moral dilemma. Should he do the right thing and report the corpse to the police and leave the crime scene unspoilt? He liked to believe himself driven by a desire to do the right thing. But he also liked the idea of earning £30K and getting a chance to drive a super-attractive sportscar. More importantly, he wanted to get this repossession resolved so he could get on with the more personal case of hunting for Fred October.

"Screw it," Dave decided.

He stepped toward the Pagani and the glint of something metal and shiny caught his eye hanging from the concierge's waistcoat pocket. It was a small model of a racing car, a miniature replica of the vehicle by his side that was being used as a key fob, and Dave carefully retrieved it. He found himself holding the keys to the vehicle and realised this discovery meant his decision had been made about whether or not to repossess the Pagani. He opened the door, climbed behind the driver's seat and, after only a moment, he was speeding out of the garage and heading toward Manchester and his £30K pay-out.

Dave thought about calling the authorities to tell them about the unfortunate death of the concierge and the seagull but the idea didn't stay in his mind for long. He worried that there might be a way of linking the Pagani to the garage. Then he fretted about the questions that would come given that he hadn't immediately alerted the police. And, finally, he consoled himself with the idea that it wasn't even a crime scene: it was just the last battleground between a man and a seagull.

With that last thought, he turned up the volume on the Pagani's sound system and tried to let the booming strains of Lynyrd Skynyrd's *Free Bird* drown out the questions that came from trying to convince himself that it was natural for a man to die during hand-to-hand combat with a seagull.

Life's a Beach

Deacon couldn't say when he woke up the following morning because he wasn't sure he'd been to sleep. He'd collapsed into his bed, aching from the exertion of removing the metal from the body of a woman he knew as Ellie who'd died under the name of Georgina Foreman. The toll of that chore had been physical, because Georgina had not been lightweight. But there was also a mental toll. He was not used to taking a Bowie knife and using it to remove piercings from corpses, or to extract amalgam fillings from a dead woman's mouth. It didn't help that Georgina had once suffered a broken leg that was splinted with an intermedullary nail. The metal-detecting scanner had wailed when it encountered this and the subsequent need to remove the metal had given Deacon a chance to find new material to fuel his nightmares. He'd had to cut the flesh from Georgina's left thigh, hack through the pale skin, the yellow fat, and the dark pink muscle, before using the Bowie knife's serrated edge to saw through the bloody-white bone.

It had not been a pleasant task.

Nor was the task made easier by the fact that Big Charlie and Annabelle were both yelling at him to hurry the fuck up because the tide was starting to turn. They were more than 500 metres away from the promenade. This was the typical distance the tide reached before coming back to reclaim the beach, and neither Annabelle's Cat nor Big Charlie's van were going to stand much of a chance at returning to the shore if they were caught by the swiftly incoming water.

Deacon stripped the last of the metal from Georgina's body, taking most of the femur out as it had grown attached to the titanium rod. He then dragged the mutilated corpse to the impromptu grave that Annabelle had cut with her Cat. There was already a rush of seawater filling the trench and Deacon felt, with dropping the woman into the hole, he was committing a final despicable act of desecration. There was enough moonlight on the beach for him to see her face in the grave, blindly staring up at him, as the seawater filled the trench and covered her damaged body. The lower half of her mouth hung open where he had been a little overzealous in using the knife to extricate her fillings.

This was the image that kept returning to him now, whenever he closed his eyes. He felt sure that he was never going to sleep again with this memory threatening to haunt his dreams forevermore. The thought brought the taste of bile to the back of his throat and pushed him close to the brink of dry-heaving.

He had turned away as Annabelle used the Cat to push excavated sand over the corpse, burying it forever. He tossed his carrier bag of Georgina's metalwork into the rear of Big Charlie's van, slammed the door closed, and then started trying to climb into the passenger side of the vehicle.

The driver was having none of that. He held up a large hand in a stop gesture and shook his head. "Don't even think about getting in here," Big Charlie told him.

"Why not?" Deacon demanded.

"You're soaked in seawater, sand and blood," Big Charlie grunted. "The first two of those items will make my van as scruffy as fuck. The last of those is going to drop so much DNA evidence in here I might as well drive straight to the police and sign a confession."

"You want me to get in the back?" Deacon exclaimed indignantly. The back of the van was the filthy haven where the corpse had been stored. He couldn't imagine a greater indignity than being consigned to becoming a passenger in the rear of Big Charlie's shitty Transit van.

"No," Big Charlie told him. "I don't want you to get in the back. I want you to get in the sea. I want you to rinse the majority of blood from your clothes. And then I want you to walk back to your home and burn those clothes just to be on the safe side. You can do any or all of those things. Or you can do none of those things and make yourself a target for the police. Ultimately, that's your choice. But, I don't want you getting in my vehicle."

Deacon tilted his jaw. It had been a difficult night and he wasn't sure he deserved to be treated with such brutal indifference. He'd provided the challenger that beat Georgina Foreman. He'd won a couple of grand at the Punch and Jodie show and he'd even mutilated a corpse in the name of helping to dispose of evidence.

Surely, he thought, those actions meant he deserved a little bit of respect and consideration. He glared insolently at Big Charlie and asked, "What if I insist on getting into this van?"

"If that happens," Annabelle said, stepping up behind him, "I'll taze you in the balls, and we'll leave you laying helpless on the sand whilst the tide comes in."

Deacon hadn't heard her approach.

He turned to see she was wielding a bulky black contraption, a contraption that he assumed was a taser, and pointing it in the direction of his balls. The idea of suffering such pain was enough to make him take a defensive step back whilst he used his hands to cover his groin.

"Trust me," Annabelle said. "If you get tased in the balls, you're going to fall to the sand and you'll count it a blessing when the tide comes in and drowns you."

From the way she was smiling as she spoke, Deacon had no difficulty believing her words to be true.

"Is the Cat secured?" Big Charlie asked her.

"We're ready to go," Annabelle said, slipping past Deacon and stepping into the van. She closed the door, dropped him a condescending wink, and then the van sped quickly off into the night, headed back to the seafront. Deacon glanced down at himself and conceded his hands were sticky with the remains of Georgina's drying blood. It was difficult to tell in the moonlight but he thought his sleeves were bloodstained up to the elbows and there looked to be dark, bloody patches on the knees of his jeans. It made sense to take Big Charlie's advice and wade into the sea but he did this reluctantly and with trepidation. It meant his trainers would be fucked and he had to hold his phone protectively out of the water so that the vulnerable technology didn't get screwed by an impromptu saltwater bath.

By the time he climbed out of the water, sodden and shivering, his mood had darkened to a hatred for Big Charlie, Annabelle and even Jodie. He stormed angrily back to the seafront and headed home via a route of sideroads and back alleyways. When he finally got into his apartment he stripped the clothes from his body, dumped them in a black binbag, and then hurled his shivering body under a scalding shower. It was only after the shower that he allowed himself to fall into bed, hoping the nightmare experience was finally over.

Maddeningly, the nightmare had continued as he tried to sleep, with Georgina's destroyed face coming back to him repeatedly whenever he closed his eyes. Around noon, deciding that sleep wasn't going to happen now, he climbed out of bed and dragged his naked arse into the kitchen. As he was making himself a reviving cup of Nescafe, he saw his phone was flashing to indicate there was a message waiting for him. He scrolled through the options and played the voicemail message from Jodie's number.

"Big Charlie and Annabelle say you were hands-on helpful last night," Jodie began without any preamble. "Come down to my nightclub. I've got the money I owe you and a chance for you to earn some more if you're interested."

Deacon glared at the phone with an expression of horrified disgust. In order to earn the money she legitimately owed him, he'd been forced to mutilate a corpse, help with its disposal, almost die from hypothermia and then have his prospects of peaceful sleep shattered for ever. He dreaded to think what he would need to do to earn money from Jodie. But he also feared the consequences of refusing such an invitation. Gingerly, he reached for the phone and returned Jodie's call.

Cock and Bull Story

Kitty took a slow walk along Talbot Road, throwing crumbs idly to the ground whenever she passed a seagull. It was early in the afternoon and most of the town's gulls had completed their daily business by this point of the day, but there were still enough birds around to make her feel comfortable with her journey. She could see two or three of them on rooftops. There was one sitting atop a rubbish bin, securing the contents like a diligent sentry. Another lazily strutted down the centre of the road, forcing cars to slow and honk impatient horns, whilst he marched onward oblivious to the delays he was causing. Seeing so many of her feathered friends within earshot, Kitty felt as though she had guardian angels accompanying her and she knew, as long as there were gulls nearby, she would always be safe.

The thought made a smile creep across her features. She clutched the silver seagull trinket in her pocket a little more tightly.

"Seagull lady!" shrieked a small child. "It's the seagull lady!"

Kitty turned and glared but did not gesture for the gull she had just fed to take any form of retribution. Sometimes it was easier to follow Christ's teachings and suffer the little children and this occasion seemed like a prime example of that truism. She didn't like being called 'seagull lady' but she also didn't want to earn the reputation of the woman who stood and watched as a flock of menacing birds pecked a toddler to death. Trying to twist her sneer into a smile of grudging acceptance, she turned her back on the child and continued on towards The Cock and Bull.

"Seagull lady!" the child called again. "She's the seagull lady!"

Kitty turned back and glanced at the little shit. It was a golden-haired cherub with cheeks so rosy they looked potentially infectious. In one hand it held an ice-cream whilst the other hand was stretched out and pointing at Kitty. The child stood outside a bookmaker's, presumably waiting on a delinquent parent, and raising his voice to get some of the attention that his family clearly weren't providing.

"Seagull lady!" he cried again.

Kitty glanced at the gull she had just treated with breadcrumbs. Their eyes met and a wave of understanding passed between them. This was an adult male herring gull and she could see he was a large specimen. From beak to tail feathers he was roughly two foot long. His ash grey wings, folded neatly across his back, would spread out to a span of more than five foot when he took flight. When the gull's gaze met hers, Kitty flicked an accusatory glance toward the child chanting 'seagull lady' and the gull nodded agreement.

Kitty turned away, not wanting any passer-by to associate her with the child's shrill, insulting cry and the fate that was about to befall him.

The gull spread its wings with a majestic flourish. It took three waddling steps in the direction of the child and then it was airborne. The toddler was no longer crying 'seagull lady' with every breath from its lungs. Instead, it was staring with wide-eyed horror as the surprisingly large bird bore down on him.

A man stepping out of the bookmaker's shrieked as the creature swooped past him. For an instant it looked like he would try and save the child. Then, with a clear choice made in favour of self-preservation, he ducked back into the shop and let the gull glide past him.

The child's eyes were fixed on the impending bird.

Kitty dared to glance back and watched the dark patch spread across the boy's groin as he pissed himself with fear. She could understand this reaction. The seagull was imposing and targeting its prey with merciless accuracy. When the gull pushed its face forward at the toddler and snatched the ice-cream from his fingers, the child let out a scream that echoed along the entire street. Kitty grinned, knowing the child could not have sounded more pained if the gull had torn a hole through his cheek.

She was still chuckling at the echoes of that tortured scream as she approached the doorway to The Cock and Bull. It was an unassuming entranceway that opened on a set of swiftly descending stairs. Music from the underground rooms thumped up to street level, making her question if she really wanted to go inside. Knowing that she had to attend this meeting, knowing that there was no way to shirk this responsibility, Kitty drew a steadying breath and stepped out of the sunlight and into the shadows of the pub's stairwell.

The Cock and Bull was stupidly loud and, even from the top of the staircase, she could sense that it stank of beer and sweat. Walking slowly down the stairs that led to the underground bar, Kitty felt as though she was entering a den of iniquity. She clutched onto the stair's handrail with a trembling grip and made her way warily downwards.

She didn't like The Cock and Bull for several reasons. The loudness disturbed her. The stench of alcohol and sweat turned her stomach. And the atmosphere of potential violence made her skin prickle with unease. Worse, and this was probably the real reason why she disliked the venue so much, the underground location meant that she couldn't be accompanied by any of her guardian angels. Instead of having the reassurance of the gulls at her beck and call, she would be entering the pub on her own.

There was a doorman at the bottom of the stairs who regarded her doubtfully. He was a broadly built man with skin the colour of midnight. "Are you sure you're in the right place, love?" he asked. "There's no bingo down here. This venue might be a bit loud for you."

Kitty reached the bottom of the stairs, withdrew her hands from the rail, and then stiffened her shoulders as she turned to face the doorman. "I want to see Jodie," Kitty told him. She nodded at the closed door behind the doorman and asked, "Is she in there?"

The doorman blinked and stepped back a little before nodding agreement. "Yeah. Jodie's in there," he allowed. "Do you want me to take you through to her?"

"I can make my own way there," Kitty said, pushing through the door and walking past him.

The doorman grunted mirthless laughter, seeming amused by her directness.

She silently cursed him as an arsehole, and scoured the room to see if she could see Jodie.

"Your bird's here," someone called.

The words were followed by a guffaw of hurtful laughter and Kitty realised this was a cruel joke at her expense. One of the young drinkers in The Cock and Bull had decided to insult one of his friends by suggesting she, Kitty, was his girlfriend: his bird. The jibe was a harsh insult for the young, afternoon drinker but it was even more damning for Kitty as she realised, because of her age and tired looks, she was now the punchline of such a malicious comment.

"At least *his* girlfriend isn't inflatable," Kitty spat, making sure her words were loud enough to be heard over the thump of a deafening base beat.

The man who'd insulted her stared as though he'd been slapped.

His friends roared with laughter.

Kitty decided to build on the theme. "At least he's got a cock that would make a woman feel it at the back of her throat," she told the man who'd insulted her. "And not something that would make her think she was flossing."

The raucous laughter grew louder as her insulter's cheeks darkened with rage. She walked past the barrage of laughter that was now directed at him and headed toward the bar where Jodie sat.

It was not difficult to find her. Even though the woman had a black baseball cap pulled down over her face and wore the collar of her black jacket turned up, Kitty recognised her immediately. Jodie was sitting right at the end of the bar, in her usual seat, with a burly bouncer standing by her side. She had been tinkering with a mobile phone as Kitty approached and, when Jodie spoke, she did so without looking up.

"What the fuck do you want?"

"I want my Bill."

Jodie shook her head. "I'm still using him."

"You told me, if I gave you £10,000, you'd set him free."

"Have you got £10,000?"

Kitty had been holding an Asda carrier bag in one hand. She dumped it on the bar beside Jodie and said, "There's £10,000 in that bag. Can I please have my Bill, now?"

Jodie glanced into the carrier bag and arched a single eyebrow. Without a second thought, she lifted the bag and dropped it behind the bar where it fell with a clatter. "The price has gone up," she decided. "Bill is proving profitable for me. I'll want at least another £20,000 from you before I let him go."

Kitty's features hardened. "You told me £10,000."

"That was a month ago when I thought that was all he was worth." She sipped at her drink for a moment before saying, "Since then, I've found out he's worth a lot more."

"But I don't have another £20,000," Kitty complained.

Jodie shrugged indolently. "Then it looks like you don't have Bill."

Kitty pointed a wavering finger at the woman. "Don't mess with me, young lady," she said firmly. "I won't tolerate this sort of treatment."

Jodie finally deigned to lift her head so the woman could see her face peering from beneath the brim of her cap. "Are you threatening me?"

"Yes."

Jodie blinked as though she had been slapped. She clearly hadn't expected this sort of response and said, "Well, don't."

"If I get you another £20,000," Kitty began. "Do you promise that you'll return Bill to me?"

"You'll need to get it to me in the next thirty hours," Jodie told her. "Bill's going to be having another fight tomorrow night and he's going up against some stiff competition."

Kitty opened her mouth to protest but Jodie shook her head and shut her down with a dour frown. "Tomorrow night Bill's going up against a new contender who's younger, faster and far more likely to win. I'm not saying the result is a foregone conclusion. But I will say: my money is not going on Bill."

"£20,000?" Kitty said quietly. She glanced at the clock above the bar and did a quick mental calculation. "And you want that by eleven o'clock tomorrow evening?"

Jodie shrugged. "I don't care either way," she said carefully. "Bring me £20,000 and you can have him. If you fail to bring the money, I'll still be in profit by the end of the day." Her smile turned bitter as she added, "But, if you want him alive, you need to act swiftly because I'm not so sure he'll make it through tomorrow night's fight."

Kitty fixed her with a long and lingering stare.

Jodie lowered her head, her attention returning to the mobile phone that hadn't left her hand. "Now, fuck off, seagull lady," Jodie said quietly. The wail of the pub's music was deafening but Kitty heard the words as though they'd been whispered into her ear. "Fuck off, seagull lady," Jodie repeated. "Or I'll have my bouncer here carry you out of this pub and throw your brittle old body up the stairs out of here."

Kitty continued to stare for a moment longer. "£20,000," she said eventually. Then, with a snort of contempt, she turned on her heels and walked briskly out of The Cock and Bull.

Hobo-Sexual

Dave was woken by the train conductor gently shaking his shoulder and telling him that he had arrived at Blackpool North. "You were out like a light," the conductor laughed. "And you were bloody lucky no one snatched your briefcase."

Dave's heart skipped a beat and he immediately reached for the Samsonite that had been given to him by one of Lloyd's Manchester-based colleagues. It was still there and, because it was a Samsonite, he figured the case was uncompromised and the contents would be secure. Placing a hand on his chest to calm himself down, he thanked the conductor again, wiped a trickle of drool from the corner of his mouth, and climbed unsteadily to his feet.

The drive to Manchester had not been arduous. The Pagani had been a pleasure to operate and, despite the fact that it hurt to make the admission, he had begun to feel agreement with the opinion of Jeremy Clarkson. He had parked the car at the location given by Lloyd and met a man who said he would transfer money to Dave's bank account. Not wanting an electronic money transfer, Dave had said he would wait until the remuneration could be given to him as a cash payment. He then spent the day in Lloyd's Manchester office, waiting to receive the Samsonite briefcase he now owned, filled with £30,000.

The good thing about a cash payment was that it was income he could hide from the taxman. The downside about a cash payment was that it could all be lost if he had the money in a briefcase and fell asleep with it whilst travelling on public transport. Marvelling at his own stupidity, not wanting to think how close he had come to losing a sum that was more than his entire income from the previous year, Dave clutched tight at the briefcase and shambled from the train and into Blackpool North station.

He bought a copy of the Blackpool Evening Gazette from the station's newsagent, intrigued by the headline that a local councillor had died after running into the path of a seafront tram. He was trying to read the article when he stepped outside the station and headed towards the taxi rank. A couple of tramps were lurking by the doors to the station, clearly trying to beg spare coppers from distracted travellers as they arrived in the town. Dave recognised Jimmy the Limp with his bright red cap and, instead of claiming a taxi, he walked over to him.

"Did you find Fred?" Jimmy asked.

Dave blushed. "I got as far as the Sally Army doors and then got called away to another job. There was a guy down there telling me he'd headed up North Shore. Does that sound right to you?" He wanted to say he'd heard some mention of the Punch and Jodie show, but he didn't want to think that sort of nonsense had started again.

Jimmy nodded. "I'd heard a handful of lads were headed up North Shore for a change of scenery. I think your Fred might have been one of those lads."

"Whereabouts in North Shore?" Dave asked.

"There's talk of lodgings being made available at the Majestic Hotel," Jimmy explained.

Dave digested this, trying to remember where the Majestic Hotel was situated. If he had his bearings correct, it was a rundown Edwardian building on the promenade overlooking the Irish Sea. He seemed to remember it was north of Red Bank Road, where the seafront illuminations concluded. "What's so appealing about the Majestic?"

Jimmy shrugged. "It's a new location," he explained. "And new locations always get a lot of interest during the first couple of weeks." He lowered his voice conspiratorially and added, "There's also talk about this place offering a little bit more, if you know what I mean?"

"No," Dave said, shaking his head. "I have no idea what you mean." He didn't know if Jimmy was alluding to sex, drugs, alcohol or some other idealised benefit that came from staying at the Majestic. His knowledge of what appealed to the homeless was close to negligible and he figured the owner of the Majestic could be giving out dogs on strings and that might be enough to entice an exodus of new patrons to the establishment.

"It's run by a woman," Jimmy explained, giving Dave a conspiratorial wink. "She's called Jodie."

Dave continued to smile, trying to work out how this piece of information related to anything else he had heard. The name Jodie made him think of the Punch and Jodie show, but he was still trying to crawl out of the fug of sleeping on the train and his mind was slow at making the connections.

"It's run by a woman?" he repeated. "Does that make it better?" he asked doubtfully. "Or does that just mean she never parallel parks outside the place?"

"They say she's on the lookout for a specific kind of man," Jimmy explained. He licked his lips and his eyes glinted with a suggestive gleam. Dave had never felt more physically repulsed by any gesture in his entire life. "She likes them muscular," Jimmy the Limp explained. "And she likes them capable of handling themselves. I think your friend Freddie Four-fingers falls into that category. Don't you agree?"

Dave was still frowning. "Are you suggesting this woman has lodgings for the homeless and she cherry-picks her customers because she has a thing for physically fit tramps?"

"She wouldn't be the first I'd heard of with that fetish," Jimmy assured him.

"She's a hobo-sexual?" Dave said, trying not to laugh at the idea. He had heard of some creepy fetishes in his life. He had heard of guys who were into watersports and women who liked the rougher side of BDSM. But he didn't think he'd ever heard of anyone fetishizing about tramps. He supposed it wasn't beyond the realms of possibility. He raised a sceptical eyebrow. "She fucks tramps?"

Jimmy was frowning. "It happens," he said churlishly.

Dave shrugged. He pulled a handful of coins from his pocket and offered them to the tramp. "Thanks, Jimmy," he said, once the money had disappeared into the other man's pocket. "I'll check out the Majestic tonight."

"He might not want to leave there," Jimmy warned. "Especially if he's getting something special from this woman owner."

"I'm not trying to make him leave," Dave assured Jimmy. "I just want to give his family some reassurance." He stepped into one of the waiting taxis and told the driver to take him home first, and then onto the Majestic Hotel. It was only when he was sitting in the back of the taxi that he remembered why the name of the Majestic Hotel was familiar. That was when he realised his investigation was a potentially dangerous one.

The Little Chef

Jodie counted the notes into his hand. The agreement had been for a straight £2,000 but she gave him £3,000. Deacon frowned at the overpayment and tried to correct the error. "This is more than you owe me for Cheryl," he said.

"You went on that disposal trip with Annabelle and Big Charlie," Jodie reminded him. "Big Charlie tells me that you were very efficient in the way that you helped."

The words glossed over the enormity of his actions. The words did not allow him to think about the fact that he'd mutilated a corpse in the moonlight beside an incoming tide. They brushed over his involvement in disposing of a body. They didn't hint at the fact that he'd nearly died from hypothermia and had an hour long walk through the night: cold, wet, fearful that he was about to be arrested, and more mentally scarred than he'd ever feared possible. Instead, Jodie's cheerful words made it sound as though he had helped take unwanted garbage to the local tip. He supposed, in Jodie's mind, that was all he had been doing.

"Thank you," he said, folding the notes and making them disappear in the back pocket of his jeans. "It was a pleasure doing business with you."

Jodie shook her head. "This doesn't have to be an end to our relationship," she told him. "I can always make use of someone who's discreet, efficient, and capable. Maybe you could make use of the extra income?"

This was the conversation he'd been dreading. Whatever task she had in mind, he suspected it would be more demanding than the work he had done for her the previous evening. However, whilst refusing would be the safest option for his sanity, he did not think that Jodie was going to take no for an answer.

He had seen Big Charlie and Annabelle in the foyer of the Majestic Hotel. They were both imposing figures but, together, he figured they'd be formidable and indomitable adversaries. Jodie had made Deacon an offer of employment and, given the criminal nature of her work, and the way she liked to take care of loose ends, he understood that he could either accept the offer or end up buried beneath the incoming tide alongside every other corpse she'd ever put out there. He didn't believe there was any middle ground where he could politely decline after admitting that the mutilation and disposal of the previous night had left him feeling violated. If he was to make any suggestion of demurring from the offer of work, he knew Jodie would have him killed in moments.

"What do you need doing?" he asked trying to make the words sound easy and inviting.

"Can you cook?"

This wasn't a question he expected. Deacon nodded.

"I've got a kitchen through there," Jodie explained. "And I keep my male fighters in the basement."

The words made Deacon's stomach twist. The more he learned about Jodie the more he realised he was being drawn into her dark and illegal world of hobo-fighting, murder and corpse disposal. He wasn't averse to breaking the law. But there were levels of degradation he didn't want to plumb and last night had taken him way past the hardest of his hard limits.

"The fighters need feeding so they're strong enough for their bouts tomorrow and later in the week," Jodie explained. "I've got four guys in single rooms downstairs beneath the kitchen and four women in the attic rooms. You reckon you could cook for eight? Annabelle or Big Charlie will help you with the serving. Do this and you can earn a grand a week with bonuses for busy periods."

Deacon nodded. He had no option but to accept the job offer, bank the money she gave him, and find a way of escaping as soon as it was viable. Jodie took him to the hotel's kitchens: a room that was all whitewashed walls and stainless steel splashbacks. The equipment was stainless steel too and stained with grease, burns and spills. Before Deacon could take a glance at the kitchen and the contents of the pantry, Jodie was leading him to a door at the back of the room which was padlocked shut.

Jodie had a bunch of keys hanging from a chatelaine on the hip of her jeans. She used one of the keys to unfasten the lock and pulled the door softly open. Before entering the darkened space where the stairs descended, she placed a hand on his chest and said, "We have an inviolate rule for entering the basement in pairs. Never less than two people at a time go down here. Each one of these fuckers is dangerous and they've got nothing to lose. The same applies to the attic rooms."

He nodded and swallowed a lump that had appeared in his throat.

"If you're coming down here with Annabelle to feed these fuckers, I want you carrying the food."

"What will she be doing?" Deacon asked.

"She's going to work the locks and carry the taser." To illustrate what she meant, Jodie pulled a taser from a cupboard he hadn't seen at the top of the stairs. It was a bulky looking contraption that had been sitting in a charger.

"How come you need a chef?"

"This is a new opportunity that's only recently arisen," Jodie said carefully. She stepped toward the top of the stairs and gestured for him to follow.

"What happened to the previous chef?" Deacon asked.

"He's the reason that we now have an inviolate rule for entering the basement in pairs."

She pulled a light-cord, and the stairs were made bright with unexpected illumination. The light shone on walls that had once been whitewashed but were now dank and dusty with age. The smell of mould, wet and disturbing, hit the back of his throat. There were other smells, but he refused to acknowledge what they might be as he followed Jodie down the creaking stairs. She stopped at the bottom, and he found himself standing in a corridor lined with two doors on either side and a single door at the far end. The floor was carpeted with something that looked like cheap underlay. The walls were the same faded whitewash that had lined the stairwell. Now he was getting the stench of stale sweat and faeces and neither aroma helped to lighten his mood.

Jodie pointed at the closest door and said, "This is Raging Bill's guestroom."

"It's not a guestroom," a voice from the other side of the door called back. "This is a prison cell and I'm being held here as a prisoner."

"Raging Bill is a prickly character," Jodie explained. She pointed to the facing door and said, "This is where we're keeping Bill's opponent for tomorrow night: Freddie Four-Fingers." She paused and said, "It should really be Freddie Nine-Fingers, because it's only on the one hand where he's missing a finger, but I found the alliteration pleasing."

Deacon nodded as though this wasn't the most surreal conversation he'd ever had in his life. He had seen Raging Bill in action. He'd never heard of Freddie Four-Fingers.

"This door," she pointed, "holds a guy I'm calling the Terminator, because he won't give me his real name yet. And this door," she pointed to the corridor's fourth door, "holds a guy I'm calling Squid Game."

"Why do you call him Squid Game?"

Jodie grinned. "He looks vaguely Korean and I couldn't understand what he was saying when I asked him his name. Squid Game seemed like an easier label for him."

"Sure," Deacon thought. "And that doesn't sound a bit racist." Aloud, he asked, "Why have you got four fighters down here?"

"Two are for tomorrow night's fight," she explained. "Raging Bill is facing off against Freddie Four-Fingers. If either or neither of them is able to fight tomorrow, I've got understudies with Squid Game and the Terminator."

"Why might they not be able to fight?" he asked curiously.

Jodie shrugged. "I've had fighters kill themselves before today. I've had fighters get themselves injured or worse when they've tried to escape. Understudies are a blessing in those circumstances." She looked set to say more but that was when the doorbell rang.

"Damn," Jodie grumbled. "I was going to let you have a chat with one of the fighters but that might not be appropriate if we've got late night guests."

Deacon took the taser from her hand and unclipped the chatelaine from her hip. "You wouldn't be employing me if you didn't think I wasn't able to handle myself," he assured her.

"And what about my inviolate rule about only coming down here in pairs?"

Deacon shook his head. "If I was serving food, it might be worth sticking to that rule. Since I'm only getting acquainted with these folks, I think I should be safe."

Jodie was barely listening, her gaze turned up to the ceiling as though she was trying to see through the floors and learn who was calling on them so late at night. When she did shift her gaze back to Deacon she nodded easily and said, "OK. I'll leave you with the taser and my keys but I will give you a final word of warning before I go."

He smiled patiently.

"If you ever remove the keyring from my jeans again without my permission, I'll have your balls removed with a rusty breadknife. Do I make myself clear?"

Deacon's patient smile was fixed into a rictus as he nodded agreement and watched her turn around and walk up the stairs. "How deep is the shit you've got yourself involved with?" he muttered uneasily. But the question was redundant. He already knew how deep the shit was: it was deep. It was far too deep.

Hello Kitty

There was always a chance to make money whilst walking down the promenade in the illuminations, Kitty thought. But she wasn't sure there would be enough opportunities this evening for her to make the extra £20,000 she needed to save Bill. She stared at the carnival-coloured lights that shone from the Pleasure Beach, the town's century-old amusement park to her right, and she said a silent prayer that her doubts were misplaced. It was a busy night with hundreds of excited tourists sauntering along the darkened promenade, eating burgers, drinking cokes, and purchasing cheap electronic gifts from itinerant street vendors. Everyone knew that each of the cheap electronics would have stopped working before the end of the night, but no one seemed to mind. Kitty knew, in this atmosphere of excess, if there was any chance of her prayers being answered, it would come from a crowd like this. But still, she acknowledged that the chances of acquiring £20,000 were frighteningly slim.

A seagull landed on her shoulder and dropped a wallet into her hand.

Kitty muttered soft words of gratitude.

She had watched the gull take the wallet from a young father who was trying to purchase a pair of plastic light sabres from a seafront stallholder. The bird had swooped in as soon as the man's wallet appeared. It had snatched the leather out of his startled fingers, and then flown off into the sky crowing with obvious delight. Kitty had walked a few yards north from the Pleasure Beach and past the glass and concrete monstrosity that was the Sandcastle water park. She was heading towards the brightly-lit frontage of the South Pier, putting distance between herself and the angry young father who was still shouting a string of curse words at the darkening sky where the gull had last been seen.

Kitty took the money out of the wallet and counted it with shaking hands. There was £85 in cash, two credit cards and a picture of an ugly baby. She dropped the wallet, baby picture and credit cards into a convenient wastebin and pocketed the notes. She'd heard stories about people illegally using the credit cards of others but that wasn't something she knew how to do. Miserably, she thought a mere £85 was not a massive contribution to her £20,000 debt but she told herself that not all the wallets she collected would provide such a meagre reward.

Another seagull dropped a wallet at her feet.

She stooped down to collect it and found this one only contained £25 in cash. Kitty looked at the two tens and a five and found herself on the brink of tears. If Bill had been there, she knew he would have been shaking his head sadly and telling her it wasn't going to be enough. The thought brought a tear to her eye and she wiped it away with the callused heel of her cold, trembling hand.

She and Bill hadn't had much, but they'd always been good together. Just like seagulls were monogamous, mating for life and never separating, she and Bill had been childhood sweethearts and spent their lives in each other's arms. With no children coming from their union, Kitty had found herself caring for the birds that visited the garden of the council flat they shared as though the screeching gulls were her own offspring. She threw out scraps for them when she had scraps, and protectively watched over nesting couples when the birds settled on the roof of a neighbouring property.

Bill, ever the practical one of them, had spent his days scavenging for food and money and anything else that might bring them a little comfort for their small nest. Occasionally his scavenging had taken him to the wrong side of the law as he did a little burglary and occasionally sold stolen goods. When his crimes took him before a magistrate, he'd invariably spend time in prison, or be tagged with one of those chunky ankle bracelets that was provided by the Electronic Monitoring Service.

It was because of Bill's police record that the council had forced them apart. Or, to be more accurate: Councillor Andy Crawford had forced them apart.

Their house in Grange Park had been one of many that was subject for demolition during a scheduled improvement programme. Whilst Bill was in prison for handling stolen goods, and a trumped-up charge of aggravated assault, Kitty had received a compulsory relocation order. She hadn't minded the move to South Shore, even though it was something she'd had to do on her own. The new property was pleasant, and she'd been delighted to find the back garden was already home to three families of nesting gulls. The only drawback to her new home was discovered when Bill was released from prison. It was a drawback that was brought to her attention by a personal visit from Councillor Crawford.

Kitty hadn't noticed at the time of the relocation but, the tenancy agreement on her new home was for a single occupant. She had argued that Bill was her common-law-husband, and the council had no right to separate an existing couple, but that meant nothing to the belligerent councillor dealing with her case. Councillor Crawford had pointed out that she'd been moved to a decent and respectable estate where they had strict policies against housing convicted criminals.

He said 'convicted criminals' whilst glaring contemptuously at Bill. He said the words as though he was spitting something unpleasant from his mouth. At the time he had been sitting in her living room, sipping a cup of Smart Price tea from her best Royal Doulton chinaware, and acting as though he owned the house which, as a senior member of the council, she supposed was almost true.

"He can't live here," Crawford said with finality. "I won't allow it."

Crawford told Kitty he was in contact with the parole services. Because Bill was wearing an electronic monitoring device, a device that accurately tracked his movements and location with GPS technology, there would be documented evidence if Bill spent too long at Kitty's property. Crawford took pleasure in telling her that such a breach of the council's rules would constitute a parole violation and would mean Bill would be returned to prison and Kitty would have her tenancy permissions revoked.

Kitty had been outraged by this. She told Crawford he could stick his South Shore house up his arse, and that she and Bill would find private accommodation without needing the help of the council. Even when Crawford pointed out that such a response would take all the couple's meagre savings, and that it was going to be difficult to get a reputable private landlord to accept a career criminal like Bill as a tenant, Kitty had still been adamant that she was going to leave the property so she could be with the man she loved. She only changed her mind when Crawford took a glance out of her rear window and saw the nesting gulls at the back of the house.

"As soon as you've left this property," he said idly, "I'm going to have those disease-carrying feathered rats destroyed."

"You can't," Kitty had exclaimed. "There are laws protecting the birds."

Bill had placed a hand on her shoulder. He shook his head and looked obviously defeated. "You'd think there would be laws protecting the birds, but people like Councillor Crawford here usually manage to find a way to get round those laws." His smile was tight when he added, "You'd think there would be laws protecting couples like us. But it seems Councillor Crawford here knows how to twist all the rules to our disadvantage."

"But -" she started.

Bill was still shaking his head. "We're humans and he's walking all over us," he whispered. "Unprotected, those poor birds don't stand a chance against someone like him."

"What are you saying?" Kitty asked, on the verge of tears. "Are you saying you're going to do as he says and leave?"

"For now," Bill agreed. "For the sake of you and our gulls out there," he added, nodding toward the rear window. "For the sake of the greater good, I'm going to leave."

She shook her head. "But I don't want you to go."

He nodded agreement. "And I don't want to go. But it seems like Councillor Crawford isn't leaving us much choice in the matter."

Crawford grinned and finished his cup of tea. "That's right," he agreed. He pulled a card from inside his jacket pocket and handed it to Bill. "As a charitable act, I will give you this address of a hostel that's available to undesirables such as yourself."

Bill had taken the card and placed a restraining hand on Kitty's arm as she bristled at the word *undesirables*. The card gave the address for the Majestic Hotel, which, apparently, was now being used as a shelter for the homeless.

"He can't do this to us," Kitty insisted.

"He *has* done this to us," Bill said flatly. He kissed her affectionately on the cheek and said, "But it won't keep us separated forever."

Neither of them asked why Councillor Andy Crawford was persecuting them so cruelly because they both knew the answer to that question. Instead, they held each other for a moment, vowing to find a way to surmount this obstacle, before eventually going their separate ways.

★★★

On the promenade, Kitty wiped another tear from her eye and told herself there was no time for brooding on unpleasant memories. She needed to be making a better attempt to raise the £20,000 that Jodie wanted in exchange for Bill's safe return. The handful of notes she currently possessed was nowhere near enough and, although she didn't like it as a solution, she knew she would have to approach another hotel.

P.I. in the Face

"I'm looking for a guy named Freddie Four-Fingers," Dave said genially when the door was opened. "I was told he might currently be one of your service-users."

The butch-looking woman who had answered the door wore combat gear and held a half-drained bottle of Corona. She stared at him with a scowl of contempt.

"Freddie Four-Fingers," Dave said again after the silence between them had stretched on for too long. "He might be here under the name Fred Oct-" he stopped himself abruptly, remembering the client's real name. "Fred Okeborne."

"Never heard of him," the woman said. She started to push the door closed and Dave stepped forward, putting his foot deliberately between the door and the jamb.

"Is there anyone else in there who might be better informed than you?"

"Are you calling me thick?" she asked. She went from holding her bottle as though it was a drink and now brandished it as though it was a weapon. "Is that what you're doing?" she pressed. "Are you calling me a moron?"

"Yes," Dave admitted. "But I was trying to do it in a polite way, so I didn't cause offence." He saw anger flare in her eyes and tried to contain the smile of satisfaction he felt at seeing her upset. "This is important to me and it's important to Mr Okeborne's family. If he is one of your service-users-"

"I've just told you, there's no one of that name here."

"And I've been told Mr Okeborne was meant to be here," Dave said coolly. "So, either one of us has been misinformed or one of us is lying."

"You're calling me thick and a liar?" She sounded outraged. Her hands were trembling with the obvious need to attack.

Dave shook his head. "Don't act surprised," he told her. "You must have heard far worse in your day."

The woman's response was swift. She had been holding the bottle of beer by its neck. She smashed the base against the wall of the Majestic Hotel. And, as the foamy spray of her Corona splashed away with fragments of shattered glass, she was left with a jagged weapon in her hand that she pushed in Dave's direction.

However, whilst her response was swift, it was pretty much what Dave had been expecting and his response was swifter.

He sidestepped.

With one hand he grabbed her elbow and pulled her out of the hotel. It was a daring move and meant, for one unsettling instant, he was dangerously close to the wicked length of broken glass she was trying to stick in him. As she staggered artlessly down the entranceway's steps, struggling to maintain balance, Dave stepped past her and entered the hotel. He closed the door behind himself and then dropped the latch, effectively locking the butch-looking woman out of the hotel.

"Who the fuck are you?" asked a burly black man sitting alone at a table in the foyer. He was climbing slowly from his seat and, despite his bulk, he looked like the sort of practical and capable thug that would take no nonsense and accept no bullshit. "Who are you?" the man demanded. "And where's Annabelle?"

Dave figured Annabelle was the butch-looking woman. He wanted to pretend there was no such person but Annabelle chose that moment to start hammering her fists on the hotel door. Speaking over the noise she made, Dave stared at the burly black guy and said, "I'm looking for a man."

"This ain't that sort of hotel."

Dave shook his head. "I'm looking for a guy called Freddie Four-Fingers," he corrected. "Jimmy the Limp told me Freddie was dossing down here. I need to speak to Freddie."

Annabelle continued to pound her fists against the door. Dave would not let his features show that he could hear her shouts and protests. He continued to glare at the surly black guy, hoping the bastard would soon relent and point him in the direction of the room where Freddie Four-Fingers was currently sleeping.

"What's going on here?" The question came from a woman dressed in shapeless black clothes, her features hidden by the brim of a black baseball cap. She spoke with the obvious power and authority that came from being in control. "Why is Annabelle outside?" demanded the woman.

Dave guessed the question was intended for the burly black guy, even though she was staring directly at him.

"He just burst in here," the black guy explained. "I don't know who he is or why he's here."

"I'm looking for a guy called Freddie Four-Fingers," Dave said again. "Jimmy the Limp told me Freddie was dossing down here. I'm here to speak with Freddie."

"And you think the best way to do that is to burst into my hotel and lock one of my staff members outside?"

Dave could feel understanding beginning to creep over him. If this was her hotel, that meant she was the woman Jimmy the Limp had called Jodie. Jodie the hobo-sexual. Looking at her, he didn't think she appeared like the sort of person who was given to such perverse appetites, but he supposed it was difficult to tell such things from physical appearances. "Is Freddie here?"

Jodie stormed past him and opened the front door.

Annabelle stood there, still holding the glass shiv she had made and looking like she was ready to use it. She started marching briskly in Dave's direction, her intentions clear from the menacing glint in her eye, but Jodie placed a hand on her arm, stopping her.

"Why don't you go and prepare a drink for our visitor?" Jodie suggested. She turned to Dave and said, "Perhaps you'd care to sit down and have a chat with Big Charlie and myself so we can establish who it is you're looking for and make sure that you're not a potential threat to any of our service-users?"

Dave considered this for a moment before nodding agreement. It was not an unreasonable request. And, even though he suspected it was entirely bullshit, he couldn't think of a way to refuse the request. He walked into the foyer area and took a chair at the same table where Big Charlie had resumed his seat. Annabelle looked murderously angry but she clearly knew better than to argue with her boss and stormed off towards a corridor that Dave assumed lead to the back of the hotel and maybe the kitchens.

"So," Jodie said, joining Big Charlie and Dave at the table and fixing him with a guarded gaze that crept from underneath the brim of her hat. "Who are you and who are you looking for?"

Dave shook his head. "You're Jodie Crawford, aren't you?"

Jodie scowled and said nothing. The silence was as good as an admission.

"Your name was all over the Gazette's front pages last year," Dave reminded her. "There was some scandal about this hotel winning a contract for providing shelter for the homeless when it was owned by a family member of one of the councillors. You and your father were made out to be the worst sort of finance-skimming criminals imaginable. But I always knew that accusation wasn't true."

Jodie smiled tentatively.

"I always suspected you were both far worse than that," Dave told her.

Big Charlie looked set to climb out of his seat. His mouth was a thin line that showed impatience.

Jodie placed a steadying hand on his arm. "What is it you want?"

"The first thing I want is Freddie Four-Fingers," Dave explained.

"Why?"

"His family are concerned about him. They've asked me to find him and make sure he's safe. I think, whilst he's in the clutches of the local hobo-fight organiser, I couldn't honestly tell them he's safe, so I'd like to take him out of here, please."

"What was the second thing you wanted?" Jodie asked.

Dave nodded. "The second thing I wanted to do was extend my condolences for the loss of your father."

Jodie studied him with an obvious lack of comprehension. "My father's not dead. I spoke to him yesterday."

"He died this morning on the promenade," Dave explained. "He got hit by a tram." He felt genuinely aggrieved for having to deliver such terrible news. He had assumed that someone would have notified Jodie about her father's death. He'd read about it in the local newspaper, and he couldn't fathom how she was oblivious to this information. "Jesus," he muttered. "I honestly thought you knew."

Jodie glanced at Big Charlie and said, "Can you go and confirm this for me?"

"Sure," he said, climbing from his seat.

Jodie glanced behind Dave and said, "You can put him out of action now."

Dave started to turn, wondering who she was talking with, and glimpsed the shape of Annabelle's silhouette. Before he could properly turn to see what the woman was doing behind him, he heard an electric sizzle and felt the numbing pain of a taser blast hitting him in the side of the neck.

Then everything went dark.

Gull Power

"You still there, chef?"

Deacon paused for a moment before he realised he was the one being addressed as chef. He was still staring at Squid Game as the guy dangled from the makeshift noose he'd made from his belt. The worry that he might have to dispose of this corpse in the same way he had to get rid of Georgina Foreman was sufficiently daunting to make him fearful of having to handle another dead body.

"Hey! Chef! You still there?"

The words were coming from Raging Bill's door. He sounded impatient and authoritative and not the sort of person that tolerated being ignored. Even though he was locked in a small room in Jodie's cellar, he sounded like he was used to being in charge.

"I'm still here," Deacon told him. He was glaring up at Squid Game and wondering how he was going to manage the logistics of getting the dead guy down from the ceiling. Without shifting his gaze from the dead man's Korean features, he asked Raging Bill, "What do you want?"

"I want to get out of here."

"Nothing I can do about that," Deacon said absently.

"I can hear keys jangling on your hip," Bill noted. "I reckon you're selling yourself short with how you could help me. I don't just *want* to get out of here. I *need* to get out of here."

"Nothing I can do about that," Deacon said again.

"Not even if you had the right incentive?" Bill asked.

In his back pocket Deacon had three thousand pounds. He was currently working for Jodie which meant he had the prospect of a consistent lucrative income. Admittedly, it looked like he would constantly be faced with chores like this one: trying to cajole a hanged body down from the ceiling, prior to organising discreet disposal of the remains. But that seemed like a small price in exchange for the rich payday he was currently celebrating. "I'm sorry to say this, man," he drawled softly. "But I don't think you've got anything you could offer as the right incentive."

"I don't have anything on me," Bill admitted. "But there's something I've got at home that I could give you, if you help me escape."

"And what would that be?"

"My wife is Kitty Wakes," Bill explained.

"Should I know her?"

"They call her the South Shore Seagull Lady."

Deacon was shaking his head. "I don't know her."

"She controls seagulls," Bill explained. "She has the power to get them to do anything she wants."

"Right," Deacon agreed. He had decided the guy was mental: possibly one too many knocks to the head during the hobo-fights, or too much alcohol afterwards, or maybe it was something to do with his Scottish accent. Whatever the cause, he didn't think there would be any advantage in entertaining Raging Bill's delusions.

The single bed in Squid Game's small cell took up the majority of the floor space. Squid Game, Deacon did not like the racism of that nickname, had tied the belt from his pants to one of the exposed beams in the ceiling. He had looped a length of the leather around his neck and then stepped off the side of the bed and hanged himself. It looked like it had not been the clean and painless snap of a breaking neck that was so often mentioned in stories of criminal execution. This had been no swift drop with the immediate relief of a sudden cervical fracture. This had been a prolonged and tortured asphyxiation that probably took place over ten or twenty minutes. Squid Game had clearly stepped from the side of the bed. Whilst the belt around his throat tightened and stopped him from being able to take in air, he had dangled, kicked and struggled. There were scratch marks around his throat as though he had changed his mind at some point about the hanging. There were broken blood vessels in his face, turning his skin to the colour of boiled meat. His sightless eyes were bloodshot and dewy with drying tears. Standing on the bed, likely standing in the same spot Squid Game had occupied prior to stepping off the bed, Deacon felt a chill of upset tickle down his spine.

"You still there?" Bill asked.

"Yeah," Deacon said quietly. "I'm still here."

"Did you hear what I said about Kitty and her abilities?"

"Yeah," Deacon replied. "That sounds like a fascinating hobby, controlling seagulls. I can imagine she's the centre of the party circuit."

"This is why Jodie has brought me in here as a fighter," Bill explained. He seemed oblivious to the sarcasm in Deacon's voice. "She's been doing this as revenge."

"Revenge," Deacon agreed.

There was a stench coming from Squid Game that made Deacon's stomach turn. It was the stench of every night club toilet he had ever visited after the hour of midnight. It was the stink of fresh shit, so moist the cloying tang stuck to the back of his throat. Deacon tried to cover his nose, but it was already too late: the vile smell was now in him. A quick glance at the body he was meant to be removing let him see that, at the moment of death, Squid Game's bowels had relaxed.

Deacon caught himself about to dry heave as he held back the need to vomit.

Oblivious to Deacon's upset, Bill was still talking. "I'm a burglar by profession," he explained. "And I accidentally robbed Jodie's house once."

Deacon blinked at this, grateful to have something to think about that wasn't the stench of shit coming from the corpse he was trying to move. He figured it was impossible for someone to 'accidentally' rob a house. It was more likely that Bill meant he had robbed Jodie's home, not realising the place belonged to a dangerous member of a local organised crime syndicate. He didn't bother to ask for a correction or clarification.

"That must have upset her," Deacon said.

"Did you know that Jodie collected certain pieces of esoteric *objet d'art*?"

Deacon wasn't sure he knew what the words 'esoteric *objet d'art*' meant. He was certain he didn't know that Jodie collected any such things. "Like what?" he asked.

He imagined he could hear Bill shrugging. "They say she had the Damned Box for a while," he said eventually. "Experts in such matters tell me that it's a box that controls all the horrors of the world. It's a box that was owned by Shipman, Hitler, Satan, Pandora…"

"I'm betting that's never turned up on the *Antiques Roadshow*," Deacon thought sourly. As Bill continued to talk he steeled himself for the task of getting Squid Game down. The belt around Squid Game's neck had tightened so it was now buried into the skin. The flesh was dark pink above and deathly white below and Deacon did his best not to look at those details. Instead he tried to see how the end of the belt was secured to the roof beam and figured the most effective method would be to cut the tether so Squid Game could fall to the floor. This approach lacked dignity and finesse, and showed little respect for the recently departed fighter. But Deacon had been reluctant to touch Squid Game before, and now he had worked out that the man had shat himself at the moment of death, he was even less eager to handle the corpse. He pulled a knife from his pocket and pressed it against the leather that hung from the beam.

"She had Crowley's runes," Bill was saying. "And a collection of occult books that cover three millennia of writing on the supernatural."

"I never knew she was a collector," Deacon said absently as he rocked the blade back and forth against the leather. "It's amazing that you can work alongside someone and not know that they've got such unusual passions."

"She also had the silver gull," Bill explained. "I took that because I thought it would be worth a few quid in scrap value. It turns out it was worth a lot more than its scrap value."

"What's the silver gull?" Deacon asked.

"It's a model of a seagull, but it's made of silver."

Deacon's blade cut through the length of leather and Squid Game's body fell with a briskness that was disturbingly swift. He landed heavily on the floor and, to Deacon's ears, it sounded like someone dropping a massive sack of potatoes from a great height.

"You alright out there, boy?" Bill asked.

"I'm OK," Deacon said. Mentally backtracking to Bill's comments from before the body fell he said, "You were telling me about this silver gull."

"Yeah," Bill remembered. "It's a model of a seagull. It's made of silver."

"I'd guessed that part," Deacon said, climbing down from the bed and trying to work out how best to now move Squid Game. "The clue was in the name. What's so special about the silver gull?"

"It's the silver gull," Bill said simply. He spoke as though he was reiterating common knowledge. "Whoever controls the silver gull controls the seagulls."

"You're going to have to say that again," Deacon said apologetically. "I'm not sure I understood."

"Whoever controls the silver gull controls the seagulls," Bill repeated. "I gave it to Kitty and she's been using it to our advantage ever since."

"What advantage is there in controlling seagulls?" Deacon asked. "At best you can steal chips from tourists and shit on parked cars. It's not exactly Thor's Mjolnir or Arthur's Excalibur, is it?"

Bill laughed darkly. "I once thought that. But that was back when I was an idiot, like you. The person who controls the gulls has the world at their command. Seagulls can steal for you. Seagulls can kill for you. Seagulls can keep your enemies at bay, and they can make your friends worship you for being their protector."

"Who are you talking to?" Big Charlie demanded.

Bill fell silent.

Deacon said, "I was just chatting to myself whilst I got this guy down from where he was hanging." He glanced up to see Big Charlie and Annabelle were coming down the stairs, manhandling an unconscious body between them. "Who's this?"

"This is Squid Game's replacement," Big Charlie explained.

"We're going to stick him in there," Annabelle said, nodding at the room where Deacon stood. "And then the three of us are going to go out and dispose of Squid Game."

Deacon nodded agreement and wondered how soon he would be able to escape from this new hell he was currently experiencing. The timeframe was unclear but he knew, no matter how quickly it happened, it could not be quick enough for him.

Flipping the Bird

Kitty had managed to get the first £10,000 from the owner of the Cleveleys Hotel. Admittedly, he was no longer in a position to help with her finances since she'd sent members of her flock to silence him. But Kitty now understood that most hotels were places that kept substantial amounts of money close to hand, and she didn't see why she couldn't prove just as persuasive to any hotelier on the promenade as she'd proved to the owner and concierge of the Cleveleys Hotel.

She was close enough to Station Road so that she could go to one of the smaller hotels that sat just off the promenade. This meant walking past a busy café, a couple of ice cream vendors and a loud amusement arcade, each of which could have proved a source of revenue. But, judiciously, Kitty figured the hotel was going to be more lucrative. The amusement arcade would likely have more money on hand, but arcades were often run by people who were familiar with threats of violence and knew how to respond to such challenges and she didn't want to run the risk of being stopped before she'd accumulated the £20,000 that Jodie had demanded.

The first hotel that caught her eye was a weary-looking building with the somewhat incongruous name of St Moritz Hotel. It was three storeys high with a ground floor bar and signage that said it was licensed to serve alcohol. Looking through the front window, Kitty could see a dozen or more tired holidaymakers playing bingo in the small main room. They wore the expressions of people who were enduring another interminable evening of forced holiday fun.

Kitty raised a hand and pointed at the hotel.

The sky was in the darkening stages of twilight, with the promenade's illuminations managing to bleach some of the night from the sky. At Kitty's command the manmade twilight briefly darkened as a flock of gulls climbed from the heavens and descended on the St Moritz Hotel. Groups of them gathered in front of windows on the upper floors and she knew there were individual birds making for the building's rear entranceways.

Her chicks were nothing if not obedient.

The thought made a smile crack across her dried and wrinkled lips. Kitty straightened her shoulders and walked up to the hotel. She pushed open the door, steeled herself for the impending confrontation and stepped inside. She had a seagull on each shoulder.

The bingo caller was just checking a winning claim as Kitty entered the hotel's bar. Inside the room she could see there were nearly two dozen people: a couple of them sipping indolently at flat pints whilst the others waited with obvious impatience to learn if the bingo winner's claim was legitimate. The prize, sitting by the side of the caller's desk, was a half-bottle of Johnny Walker, so Kitty could understand why the tension was so high.

The room was typical of every hotel bar she had ever visited in the town.

There was a window at one end of the room which, if a customer sat in just the right position, would allow them sufficient glimpse of the beach to call it a sea view. Facing the window was a modest bar, a quarter of the size of a real bar but with drinks at three times the price. The walls on one side of the room were lined with chairs surrounding a dance floor that was large enough for three couples – maybe four if they were all anorexic. On the other side of the dance floor there was a small podium for singers, comedians and, on this evening, a bingo caller. A slowly revolving mirror-ball above the dance floor made the hotel bar identical to every other one Kitty had ever visited.

The landlord, standing behind the bar, looked up as Kitty entered. The room was silent as they waited for the bingo-caller to finish checking the winning card and the tension in the air was sudden and disturbing.

"What do you want?" the landlord asked.

Kitty regarded him with cold eyes. "Money," she said simply. "I want £20,000 to be exact."

The landlord shook his head. "It doesn't work like that in here. No one comes into my hotel begging for money."

Kitty shook her head. "I'm not begging," she assured him. "I'm demanding payment with malice."

The landlord frowned. He started toward the end of the bar where she could see a baseball bat was propped in a corner beside the till. Along the length of the baseball bat someone had printed in calligraphic script: *the management's decision is final.* The calligraphy had been done in a red ink that was so vibrant it seemed to hover above the wood. "You're demanding money?" the landlord repeated.

Kitty nodded.

The customers in the bar were shifting their gaze from the landlord to Kitty like the crowd at a tennis match. When they saw her nod to the admission that she was demanding money, they all turned to see how the landlord would respond.

"That's not funny," he said, reaching for the baseball bat. "Get out of my hotel."

Kitty pointed at a woman who had been standing behind the bar beside the landlord, working as a barmaid. She was a busty blonde with too much cleavage and bright red lipstick. She had been watching the exchange with obvious uncertainty. Now, finding herself the centre of Kitty's attention, she looked distinctly unsettled.

"Her," Kitty cawed.

The gull on Kitty's right shoulder responded immediately. It gave a screech like murder and sped from her shoulder with disturbing velocity. The busty barmaid opened her mouth in shock but there wasn't time for the woman to step backwards or even raise her hands in self-defence. Kitty's gull buried its beak into the barmaid's right eye.

And pandemonium erupted.

The barmaid released a scream and fell backwards. Blood was gushing from her eye-socket. The landlord looked like a man who wanted to intervene but he was hesitating with his hand unable to squeeze around the baseball bat. Kitty couldn't tell if he was hesitating because of the blood he had just seen, because he had a fear her gull would turn on him, or if he was simply too confused to act. Whatever the reason, he lurched from one foot to the other, glancing at Kitty, the gull, the barmaid, and his excited customers.

The excited customers were adding to the chaotic spirit of mayhem.

They had been sitting quietly in the modest bar, waiting for their bingo game to resume, sipping on overpriced drinks, and enjoying the spectacle of the South Shore Seagull Lady arriving and causing a scene. Now, urged on by the shriek and wail of the partially blinded barmaid, panic seemed to have ensued. Some of them were headed for the bar's exit and Kitty sent her other gull to guard the door.

"No one leaves here until I've got my £20,000," she told them. Someone moaned.

The landlord finally found the courage to grab his baseball bat and, holding it in both hands, stepped boldly from behind the bar.

Kitty's first seagull leapt at his face. Part of its chest was stained red with blood from the barmaid. Other than that discolouration of its feathers, the bird seemed relatively unscathed from the assault it had just performed and had no problems fluttering across the bar and fixing its beak around the landlord's ear.

He screamed.

Kitty could understand the man's cry. Gulls had an impressive bite and because of their tomia, the ridges of cutting edges within their mandibles, they were able to grip with surprising tenacity. Right now the gull had hold of the landlord's ear and was flapping determinedly backwards to allow the movement to shred skin and cartilage.

The landlord dropped his baseball bat and tried to beat at the bird with his hands.

Somewhere above them Kitty heard the shatter of breaking glass and the screech of frightened tourists. She snapped her fingers and the gull stopped biting at the landlord and flew back to her shoulder.

As Kitty stepped to the centre of the dancefloor, she waited as confused and terrified guests of the St Moritz stumbled into the bar, ushered there by brutal seagull guardians who had harried them from their rooms and down the stairs.

"What the hell do you want?" the landlord gasped. He held one hand over his bleeding ear and glared at Kitty with a hatred that was almost overwhelming. "What are you doing in my hotel and what do you want?"

"I've already told you what I want," Kitty reminded him. "Weren't you listening? I want £20,000." Her voice was soft enough to make them all fall silent as they strained to hear her demands. Kitty glared at everyone in the room and said, "I'm sure, between you all, you can manage that, can't you?"

"My eye," wailed the barmaid. "It took my eye."

No one bothered to help her.

"What if we can't raise your £20,000?" the landlord asked.

Kitty gave him an inscrutable smile. "Let's cross that bridge when we get to it," she said softly. The seagull on her right shoulder squawked and that sound was enough for everyone in the bar to understand that she would have all of her money before she left the hotel.

Game P.I.

Dave came back to consciousness inside a small room that he guessed was now his cell at the Majestic Hotel. There was an exposed beam on the roof that still had a strip of belt hanging from it and he tried not to think why he would be put in a place that contained such an ominous souvenir of its dark history. If this was being done to deliberately spook him, he had to admit it was working. If he was simply being put in a room where suicide was so commonplace, that thought was even more worrying because it implied his situation was genuinely hopeless.

His head hurt like a bastard and throbbed even more when he pulled himself from the bed. He groaned unhappily and asked, "Where the fuck am I?"

"Are you the new fighter?" called a faraway voice.

"Fighter?" he wondered. That didn't sound like good news considering what he knew about Jodie Crawford. "Hello!" he called out loud. "Who's that?"

"The name's Bill. Are you the new fighter?"

Dave had never considered himself to be a fighter but, if what he'd heard about Jodie Crawford's setup was true, previous experience was not an essential prerequisite. "I don't think I'm a fighter," he admitted. "I think I've just pissed off the wrong person and landed myself in a situation."

A third voice joined the conversation. Morosely, he said, "If you've pissed off someone here, you're about to become a fighter."

"That's it, Freddie," Bill called, the suggestion of laughter at the back of his throat. "Break it to him gently."

"Freddie?" Dave called. "Fred Oct- Fred Okeborne?"

When he next spoke, Freddie sounded guarded. "How do you know me?"

"Your family asked me to look for you," Dave explained. "You went walkabout from Sheffield. They thought you might be in Blackpool. They called me to investigate."

Silence stretched between the walls.

"Does that mean someone knows where you are?" asked Bill.

Dave glared at the door, hating the question Bill had just fired at him. If he'd been any good at his job, Dave would have contacted someone – anyone – to let them know he was going to investigate a lead at Jodie Crawford's Majestic Hotel. But, because he ran his investigation agency on a minimal budget, keeping expenses as low as possible with the lowest amount of overheads, there wasn't another member of his investigating team who he had been able to trust the information of his location. In truth: there just wasn't any other member of his investigating team.

"Does this mean someone knows where you are?" Bill asked again.

"Let's not get too optimistic about someone coming to our rescue," Dave cautioned. "At the moment, I'm not sure where I am so I doubt anyone else knows."

He walked gingerly over to the door and tried the handle. It was locked. Jiggling the handle didn't help.

"It's padlocked on the outside," Bill explained, as though he had heard Dave testing the handle. "Two padlocks for each door," he added.

Dave returned to the bed and lay down. He had no problem working on padlocks when he could get to them but, if the padlocks were on the other side of the door, he figured he was secured in the room until someone let him out.

"Am I right in thinking you guys are the latest players in the Punch and Jodie show?" Dave asked.

"You've heard of it?"

"I keep my ear to the ground. How do we get out of here?"

"We don't," Fred said miserably. "We're each locked in a secure cell. The doors are only opened for meal breaks and a toilet break that comes once every three hours. The new setup is that there will be two people coming down to feed us one at a time. One of them will have the food. The other will have a taser."

Dave rubbed his still-painful neck, reluctant to think about the agony that came from being struck by a taser and unwilling to suffer that ignominy a second time. He was fairly sure he had pissed his pants when the electricity started to crackle through him.

"If all those precautions are in place," Dave asked. "Then how do we make our escape?"

Bill laughed without humour.

"You should put that thought out of your mind right now," Fred admonished. "Jodie doesn't leave anything to chance. Plus, if she hears that you're trying to make a break for freedom, she'll punish you in ways that you don't want to imagine."

Dave shook his head. Ignoring the threat of torture to which Freddie had alluded, he said, "There must be a potential way to escape." After a moment's thought, he asked, "How are you taken from here to the fight venue?"

Bill answered. "We're taken one-by-one. We're handcuffed by a pair of her bouncers from The Cock and Bull whilst either Big Charlie or Annabelle holds a taser on us. If we don't consent to being handcuffed we're tasered and the cuffs are put on whilst we're incapacitated."

"Shit," Dave muttered. The precautions taken by Jodie and her team seemed maddeningly well-considered.

"Once we're cuffed, we're thrown into the back of a Transit van," Fred explained. "Both fighters are put in the same van and secured to the panels by hooks that are already there. The cuffs are still on, so there's no chance to escape. And we're driven down to the beach."

Dave was still nodding. The little he knew about the hobo-fights had told him that some of them took place on the seashore. He tried to picture each scene that Bill and Fred had described but none of them seemed to offer him any hope of successfully breaking free. It sounded as though the journey from cell to seashore was tightly controlled and wholly inescapable.

"What happens on the beach?"

"Whilst we're still cuffed, our fists are wrapped," Bill explained. "First, they're wrapped in tight bandages. Then those bandages are wrapped with barbwire and maybe decorated with razor blades."

Dave swallowed. Each step sounded as though it had been carefully considered to stop anyone from running away from the fights.

Bill went on, saying, "We're then taken out of the van-"

"With our hands still cuffed behind our backs," Fred broke in.

"-and pushed face first into the wet sand," Bill explained.

"It's whilst we're face first in the sand that they unfasten our wrists," Fred continued. "Because there's little chance of us attacking from that position."

"Particularly with a taser wielding thug leering over us at the time," Bill agreed. He barked dry laughter and added, "And you need to be wary of that bitch Annabelle because, if she can, she'll get the taser to hit you in the balls."

"A taser to the balls is the worst," Fred agreed.

Dave wasn't really listening. He was trying to think if any of the scenarios Bill and Freddie had mentioned offered the slightest opportunity for him to fight back, take control and achieve an escape. The picture they painted was disturbingly bleak but he felt sure that there must be some chance to fight back that they were overlooking.

"During the fight Jodie has at least three guards with tasers pointed at us at all times," Bill explained. "I was in a fight where some guy floored me with a haymaker and, whilst I was staggering into the audience, he tried to make a break for it." He sucked unhappy breath through his teeth and said, "He got caught in the crossfire of three tasers. The poor bastard lit up like a Christmas tree and, when he collapsed on the sand, there was smoke coming out of his mouth."

"Jesus Christ," Dave marvelled.

"After the fight, the winner gets tasered into unconsciousness," Fred told him. "It's a short, brutal but effective way to resume control. You wake up back in your cell with your bandages and barbwire removed and a fresh set of scars that will likely never get a chance to heal before you're next involved in a fight."

"Jesus Christ," Dave said again. "You guys paint a grim fucking picture."

"Did you want us to tell you about all the fun parts and the rich opportunities for travel, adventure and escape?" Bill sneered sarcastically. "Because I'm pretty sure those things don't happen."

Dave was silent for a moment, trying to ignore the defeated tone of Bill's voice, and then said, "During the fight…"

"When we've got three guards armed with tasers waiting for us to take a step out of line?" Fred asked. "During that fight?"

Dave shook his head, wishing that the two wouldn't focus on the negative. "What would happen if one of you fell into the crowd?"

"The poor fucker would likely get tasered in the balls," Bill said. "Like we said before, that's where Annabelle usually aims for."

"Would it be enough of a distraction for the other fighter to make a break for it and run away?" Dave asked.

"Run where?" asked Bill. "These fights take place at midnight on the beach. Even if all three of the guards get sufficiently distracted by a fighter being flung into the crowd, the one of us making a break would have to run all the way back down the beach to the stairs and then run up the stairs to get to the sea defences. Even if we could climb up those slippery steps in the dark with our hands bandaged, we'd most likely be caught before we got to the promenade."

Dave thought about this for a long moment, still staring at the door of his cell and wondering if he had finally seen a way to forge an escape. He didn't think his idea was particularly original, but he did think it was a possibility that had been overlooked.

"What if you didn't go to the seafront?" Dave asked.

"Where else is there to go?" asked Bill.

"Running north or south would be a mistake," Fred told him. It's difficult running on sand and they've got a Transit with Big Charlie and Annabelle sitting behind the wheel. They'd be on top of us within seconds if we tried to go north or south."

"What if you went west?" Dave suggested. "What if you swam out to sea?"

There was silence outside the room for a moment.

"They'd never be expecting that," Bill marvelled. "They'd be searching the seafront for us, and we'd have gone in the opposite direction."

"But how far out could we swim?" Fred asked.

"You'd need to go no further than the end of the nearest pier," Dave explained. "Whichever one of you escapes can swim out to North Pier, maybe climb up the pier's supporting stanchions, and maybe use that as an opportunity to tear the bandages and barbwire from your hands. From there you just need to get to the topside of the pier and you're safe and free. Then, as soon as you feel safe enough to do it, you can go to the police and report Jodie and the

Majestic Hotel and get them to send the cavalry here to save those of us who were left behind."

"I can see that working," Bill said happily. "I really think that's a plan that could work," he declared.

"It wouldn't be easy," Fred argued. "Swimming at night, wearing jeans and with your hands bandaged: that won't be easy."

"But it won't be impossible," Bill argued.

"No," Fred admitted.

For the first time since he had heard him speak, Dave could hear a suggestion of hope in the man's voice. He grinned, pleased to think that he had been responsible for that glint of optimism in the man's tone.

"No," Fred said cheerfully. "It wouldn't be impossible."

"In fact," a woman called out from behind the door. "The only thing that could potentially spoil this plan would be if I found out what you intended to do."

Recognising Jodie's voice, Dave sighed and collapsed back on his bed.

"How long were you out there?" he asked.

"I never moved away after locking you in your room," she admitted. "So, I heard everything."

"Shit," Dave said bitterly. With a sudden suggestion of hope in his voice he asked, "I don't suppose this means you've had a change of heart about tomorrow night's fight and you're going to call it off, are you?"

There was a moment of silence outside the room before Jodie said, "As a matter of fact I have had a change of heart about tomorrow night's fight. Instead of pitting Bill against Fred in a hobo deathmatch, I'm going to have him fight you."

Dave thought she might have said more but, at that moment, he heard someone pounding on the front door and he knew there conversation had come to an end.

Somewhere Beyond the Sea

With a disquieting sense of premonition, Deacon realised, if he didn't do something proactive, he would one day be a corpse in the back of Big Charlie's van, headed to a final resting place beneath the waves.

He was once again sitting between Big Charlie and Annabelle with the stench of Squid Game's shit-marinated corpse coming to him from the back of the vehicle. They were travelling a little more slowly since Annabelle had attached the Cat to the back of the vehicle and, once they were on the beach, they were simply floating through an infinite darkness that was so impenetrable they could have been parked in the deepest depths of outer space.

"You must have made a big impression on Jodie," Annabelle observed. "She doesn't usually take people into her confidence so quickly. Yet here you are trusted as the Little Chef."

Deacon shrugged, unable to think of a witty response to the comment. "That's me," he admitted, wishing he didn't sound so listless. "I'm the big impression maker."

His thoughts were going back to the night he had been with Cheryl and introduced her to the world of hobo-fighting. It had started off as a good night with a little bit of beer, some fun sex and a couple of effective tablets. Deacon wasn't sure why he had handed Cheryl over to Jodie. He only knew it had felt like the right decision at the time. But, ever since then, he felt as though it had been a mistake and he couldn't help wonder if it was a mistake he should try to rectify.

The thought weighed heavily on him.

No one deserved to be trapped as one of Jodie's prisoners, kept in a cell and used as the centrepiece in a violent deathmatch. Cheryl particularly didn't deserve that as she had laughed at his jokes, made him feel like an attractive and desirable guy, and he had sold her down the river.

Big Charlie brought the van to a halt mere yards from the incoming tide.

Deacon was out of the door as soon as Annabelle had moved and he was rushing to the rear of the vehicle. He had taken what he needed from the glove compartment and had the metal-detecting paddle in one hand and the knife and carrier bag in the other as he dragged Squid Game's body from the back of the van.

"Do you need a hand with that?" Big Charlie asked.

Deacon shook his head. "You do your thing," he called absently. Without thinking about his actions, he pulled off his hoodie and placed it on the damp sand. Then, unmindful that Big Charlie and Annabelle were nearby, he started to tug off his trainers, socks, and jeans. By the time he was finished he was completely naked with his clothes folded into a neat pile a few yards away from Squid Game's corpse.

Both Big Charlie and Annabelle were watching him with expressions of doubt and curiosity. From the cabin of the Transit van, Big Charlie called, "You ain't going to fuck it, are you?"

"Neither of us want to see that, if that's what you're planning," Annabelle assured him. "We don't fuck corpses on this job. No matter how sexy they look."

"I'm not going to fuck it," Deacon assured them, not sure he was happy that the anonymous corpse had now lost its gender and become a thing that could be described as 'it'. He wasn't happy that he didn't know the name of the dead man, and was only able to think of him in terms of the racial epithet 'Squid Game'. But the shift away from calling the body 'he' or 'him' seemed like an act of desecration that was worse than the violations he was expected to perform to render the corpse unidentifiable. "I've taken my clothes off so they don't get contaminated by any of this guy's blood, DNA or trace evidence," he explained.

Annabelle nodded. "And you're not embarrassed that we can both see your micro-penis?"

Big Charlie laughed at this comment.

The previous evening Deacon might have blushed at such an insult. He would have been tempted to cover himself, point out that the night was cold and he was naked for the sake of practicality rather than as an act of potential intimacy. Instead, he simply turned to Annabelle and told her to fuck off.

Because he was naked and holding a Bowie knife, she did as he requested.

Kneeling beside the corpse, Deacon waved the scanner paddle over Squid Game's face and found the guy had a handful of amalgam fillings that needed to be removed. The paddle crackled brightly when it went over the zip of the corpse's jeans, and it pinged around a couple of areas that might have been metallic buttons. The excess noise made Deacon realised he was going to have to strip the body to be sure of it being invisible to early morning metal-detectors.

It crossed his mind that, when he'd been presented with the corpse of Georgina Foreman, the idea of touching a dead person was enough to make him feel like vomiting. Now, even though this was only his second corpse, Deacon felt sufficiently untroubled by the experience that he was no longer thinking of Squid Game as having once been a human being. Even when he pulled the pants from the corpse, and caught the rich tang of wet shit, he wrinkled his nostrils at the brief assault, and then forgot that the stench came from something that had once been human. He reminded himself he was simply involved with destroying evidence and, the more efficiently he did that, the less likely it would be that this came back to bite him in the ass at some point in the future.

The Bowie knife was powerful enough to remove the fillings and Deacon dropped them in the carrier bag along with pieces of attached teeth. Squid Game was also wearing a cheap metal ring around one finger and, when it wouldn't come off, no matter how Deacon twisted or pulled, he was left with no choice other than to use the Bowie knife to remove the finger. The action struck Deacon as no more intense than if he had been cutting a sausage in half. The Bowie knife was wickedly sharp and, whilst he could have seen this as an act of corpse desecration, he reminded himself that Squid Game no longer had any need for his fingers and a missing one would not be a problem for where he was going.

Deacon dropped the ring into the carrier bag and then, to be sure that the finger didn't find its way to the shore where it could potentially expose Jodie or himself to a police enquiry, he shoved it into Squid Game's anus. It was this action that made him wonder what he had become. For the first time since the van had parked, Deacon felt as though he had crossed a line.

"Did you just shove something up his ass?" Big Charlie called from the Transit. "I was watching from the wing mirror and I'm sure I saw you shove something where the sun don't shine."

"He's shoving stuff up the dead guy's ass?" Annabelle repeated. She sounded amazed and horrified. She blinked down at Deacon and said, "You must have been thrilled when you found out there was work like this available to you, you fucking pervert."

Deacon didn't respond to either of them. He bundled the shit-soiled clothes, jewellery and metal fillings into the carrier bag and then dragged the naked corpse to the hole that Annabelle had made in the sand. He stood up, breathless, still naked, and unembarrassed by his nudity.

"This was a damned sight faster than last night," Annabelle muttered as Deacon hauled Squid Game into the makeshift grave.

Deacon shrugged. "I know what I'm doing now," he admitted. He went to the back of the van and dumped the carrier bag there before going to Big Charlie's side of the vehicle.

"Your cock's still out," Big Charlie noted. "And it's still fucking tiny."

Deacon handed him the paddle and the Bowie knife. "I've rinsed the blade in the sea," he said. "I'll see you back at the Majestic."

"You don't want a lift back?" Big Charlie asked, sounding surprised.

"Like you pointed out last night," Deacon said. "If I take a short swim in the sea, I can remove a lot of the evidence from my body that might link me to the corpse."

"He's starting to think like one of us," Annabelle said cheerfully. She had driven the Cat onto its trailer at the rear of the van and was climbing into the passenger side of Big Charlie's Transit.

"I don't think that's true," Big Charlie said. "Neither of us would be standing in the cold with our balls out having just shoved a finger up a dead guy's ass." His comment made Annabelle laugh and, with the sound of their merriment ringing in his ears, Deacon was left alone on the pitch-black beach with only the sound of the incoming tide and his own chattering teeth for company.

He made his way toward the sea, stepping on Squid Game's hastily filled grave, and trying not to think of the man's hand bursting through the sand and clutching at his ankle. The water was offensively cold, but Deacon made himself stay beneath the waves until the taillights of the transit had disappeared. Things touched his feet, ankles, and thighs, but he wouldn't let himself be unnerved. There was flora and fauna beneath the waves and he was 99% sure that none of those things touching him were Squid Game's dead fingers.

He had come to a decision.

As he stepped from the water he barely shivered as he reached for his clothes and began to put his sodden body into them. He was cold and dirty and had been exposed to another night of horrors that would possibly haunt his psyche for the rest of his days. But he had come to the decision that he was going to make it up to Cheryl. He was going to make it up to Cheryl and that was going to happen as soon as he had access to Jodie's female prisoners.

Charmed Lives

Jodie opened the doorway and looked only mildly surprised to find Kitty Wakes standing there, holding an overstuffed Sainsbury's carrier bag. Since she had made her demand for £20,000 that afternoon, Kitty figured Jodie had been expecting a visit and she now wondered if she was walking into a trap.

"Here," said Kitty, throwing the overstuffed carrier bag at Jodie's feet. "Here's your money. This is the £20,000 you wanted. Now give me my man."

Jodie remained in the doorway glaring warily at Kitty. She cast her scowl around the frontage of the hotel and Kitty could read the nature of the woman's suspicion.

"I've brought no birds with me," Kitty said testily. "I'm playing honestly by your rules. That's the money you demanded from me. That's the payment. Now give me my Bill."

Jodie stepped back and opened the door wide, inviting Kitty to join her in the Majestic Hotel. "Come inside," Jodie said. "Let's talk about this."

"How do I know I can trust you?" Kitty asked.

Jodie shrugged. "You probably can't," she admitted. "But if you don't come inside, you'll almost certainly never see Bill again, so you've got to do what you think is best." Leaving the door open, she turned her back on Kitty and walked into the darkened depths of the building.

Reluctantly, Kitty stepped inside and closed the door behind herself. When her eyes had adjusted to the gloom of the Majestic's interior, she saw that Jodie was sitting at a table in the hotel's foyer. She had a glass of wine in her left hand and was pouring a fresh glass for Kitty from the bottle she held in her right.

"You want me to drink with you?" Kitty asked doubtfully.

"We've never had a proper chance to talk," Jodie explained. "Too often, when we get together, either you're calling me names and threatening me with all manner of retribution, or I'm threatening to have you pushed down some stairs." She finished topping up Kitty's wine glass and said, "I figured, if we had a chat, maybe we could resolve some of our differences."

Reluctantly, Kitty sat down on the opposite side of the table in the foyer and sniffed warily at the glass of wine. It smelled fresh and crisp but that didn't mean it wasn't filled with poison. She glared at the glass whilst Jodie sipped her drink and smiled with an expression that was so smug and self-satisfied, Kitty wanted to lean across the table and drag her fingernails down the woman's face.

The silence between them stretched out until Kitty could hear the purr of the sea outside. She shifted her glare of hatred from the untouched glass of wine to Jodie's sneer of a grin.

"Where's Bill?" she asked eventually.

Jodie shook her head. "Do you know what I admire most about you?"

Kitty didn't know and didn't care. "Where's Bill?"

"He's safe," Jodie assured her. "He's safe. But answer my question. Do you know what I admire most about you?"

"Is it the fact that I can put up with your bullshit?" Kitty asked.

Jodie laughed without humour and relaxed into her chair. "The thing I admire most about you is the way you pretend you're the innocent victim in all of this," Jodie explained. Her tone hardened as she added, "You pretend you're the innocent victim in all of this, when it was your thieving boyfriend that stole the silver seagull from my father."

Kitty took a sip on her drink. "And where did your father get it from?" she mused. "Where did your noble father – a man who has always been open, honest and completely above board with all of his business dealings – where did he acquire the silver gull?"

Jodie shot her a silencing glare. It was a glare that said it was wrong to say unkind things about the dead. The scowl in her eyes was enough to tell Kitty that Jodie knew how her father had acquired the silver gull and it was clearly a truth that did not sit easily with her.

According to local legend the silver gull had been forged by an old wise woman in the 1500s. She had lived in the shoreland marshes on the Fylde coast, a little south of a location noted for a pool of water that was liver-coloured, or black, and from which the area would one day take its name: Blackpool. The wise woman created a small silver gull to celebrate the local birds that she loved so dearly. This charm was something she wore around her neck on a leather thong, and it became an heirloom that was passed down from generation to generation through a family that had an affinity with the local birdlife. The family fed the birds and provided a safe haven for them to nest and build communities. They built boundaries to keep out predators and the relationship between the family and the birds became so well known that it was said, whichever family member owned the silver gull, controlled the birds.

Kitty didn't know how much truth there was to this history, but she did know there had been stories that supported the idea. One of the early railways that came to the coast had been expected to run through the property of the bird-loving family. The family had tried to object, and made their grievance known to the local council, but all to no avail. However, when workmen started trying to lay track across the family's property, it was discovered that the gulls also objected to the development.

Two Irish labourers had been hospitalised by gull attacks. A third had lost a finger and a fourth one later died from a wound that became infected on that first attempt to lay unwanted railway lines across the property. It was said that the attacks had been watched by the matriarch of the family: an elderly woman clutching a silver bird-shaped talisman. It was also said, by the man who lost his finger, that the old woman looked like she was commanding the birds and directing them to make their attacks.

But no one believed him.

One of the people who definitely didn't believe that story was Councillor Joseph Whyte who went out to the property and argued that the birds needed destroying. He said they were dangerous. He said they were getting in the way of progress. He said they were going to be eradicated so the town could benefit from an influx of tourists and travellers who would be arriving on the new trains. He said a lot more but, before he could put his plans to murder the gulls into action, Joseph Whyte was found dead on the seafront. No one knew what had happened to him, but it looked as though he had been chased into the sea by an unidentified person, creature, or group of creatures. There were a few marks on the back of his scalp and the backs of his hands, all of which looked like the scars that would be made by a bird's beak: a gull's beak to be specific. But most people agreed that was just a coincidence and probably had nothing to do with the reason why Councillor Joseph Whyte had drowned. Whyte would have been pleased to learn that the introduction of the railway went ahead, although his pleasure might have been lessened slightly had he discovered that train accessed the small town through a modified route, and the safe haven for the birds remained a sanctuary for the bird-loving family's gulls.

The heirloom had been passed down, usually from mother to daughter, and the rumours about its ability to control gulls continued to be whispered by those who knew the family. One owner of the silver gull, a young lady who was in the unfortunate position of being promised to a man who transpired to be a drunken womaniser, was claimed to have taken matters into her own hands and had the birds help her get retribution. After a night when she had been found grievously assaulted – the subject of physical violence and, according to the more salacious stories, the suggestion of sexual assault – she told her family her injuries had been caused by her betrothed. When they advocated taking legal action against him, she refused their help and said she would deal with the matter herself.

Two days later he was found dead on the promenade.

The coroner thought he might have had a stroke whilst sitting on a bench overlooking the cliffs at Bispham. It was a kinder idea than the one that crossed most people's minds when they heard that the victim's flesh had been stripped from his face, the hair had been torn from his head and his eyes had been pecked from their sockets. He was swamped in an excited torrent of guano, which was spattered all around his remains. The young boy who found the corpse was likely scarred for life by the sight of the fleshless skull protruding from the collar of a bloodstained jacket.

And so the reputation of the silver gull had continued to grow and the heirloom had stayed within the bird-loving household until Councillor Andy Crawford found himself admiring the jewellery when he visited the eldest member of the family. It was a work visit where Crawford was assessing the woman's eligibility for social housing, and he had found himself alone in her living room whilst he waited to be brought a cup of tea.

She was a dippy old bag, he had thought, clearly a few plates short of a picnic set, and he had been surprised that she left the silver gull-shaped trinket on the arm of her chair when she left the room. He picked it up, examined it through squinted eyes, and then decided it would either make a good gift for his daughter or it might even be something he could flog to a local jeweller. Either way, the words, "Finders, keepers," were going through his thoughts as he stuffed the charm into his pocket.

★★★

"Your father stole it," Kitty said again.

Jodie was shaking her head. "Your thieving boyfriend stole the silver gull from my father and then he went and gave it to you. He's a thief. You've received stolen goods. And you both make out that you're the innocent victims in all of this."

Knowing there was nothing she could say that would meet with agreement, Kitty sipped her drink and tried to suppress her smile. It was true that Bill had stolen the silver gull from Crawford. But, because he had given it to her, she saw that as having had the charm returned to its rightful owner. The surname of the bird-loving family had been Wakes. It had been her late mother who'd had the gull stolen from her by Crawford and, because Kitty was now the eldest of the Wakes women, she believed that possessing the silver gull was her birth right.

Jodie took a sip from her wine glass and leant over the table. "Do you know why my father kept Bill out of your house in South Shore?"

"Because he was a despotic little prick with a power fetish?" Kitty suggested.

"Because he wanted you to do the right thing," Jodie growled. "He wanted you to give back the silver gull and return it to its proper owner: me."

"Pah," Kitty snapped. "You would have been a shit owner for the silver gull. You've got no compassion for the creatures."

"They're flying vermin," Jodie pointed out. "They're rats with wings. Why should I have compassion for them?"

Kitty tried to climb from her chair but Jodie leapt out of hers and hurriedly pushed her back into the seat.

"I should be the one with the power that you have," Jodie said. "Give me the silver gull and I'll let you keep this twenty grand and you can take Bill home with you tonight."

Kitty snorted in disdain. "And how long would either of us last if you had the power of the gulls?"

Jodie couldn't resist a sly smile. "I don't know what you mean," she mumbled, returning to her seat and trying to feign innocence. "Surely you don't think I would be crass enough to exact some sort of petty revenge on you?"

"You'd have us pecked to death before dawn," Kitty sneered. "You'd probably film it with that camera-phone thing of yours and watch it again and again and again."

Jodie's smile was broad enough to tell Kitty that she was correct. She was all but chuckling at the idea of such a scenario.

"But," Kitty went on, "that's not the reason I refuse to let you have the silver gull. I refuse to let you have the silver gull because I know you'd be a tyrant to those poor birds. You'd hurt them. You'd make them hurt themselves. You'd put them in situations that were dangerous. And I could never allow that. They deserve much better."

Jodie sniffed with disdain. "And you've never done anything like that?"

Kitty blushed. She lowered her gaze and tried to think of a way of refuting Jodie's accusation without sounding guilty. "I love my chicks," she said simply.

"Did you love that one that died with the concierge of the Cleveleys Hotel?" Jodie asked. "It snatched open the concierge's jugular but, before he died, he'd twisted the thing's neck." Her mean smile widened as she said, "I hear he'd almost twisted the fucking thing's head from its shoulders."

Kitty blinked back a threatening tear. "In every war, there are going to be casualties."

"Is that what this is?" Jodie asked. "Is this a war? Was it a war at the St Moritz Hotel tonight? According to my sources they're still sweeping seagull corpses out of the main bar." Her smile twisted cruelly and she asked, "Are they all casualties of war?"

Kitty's eyes widened. "How did you know about the St Moritz Hotel?"

"How did I know that you demanded money with menaces from a Station Road hotel?" Jodie scoffed. "You don't think a story about a seagull robbery wouldn't make the news? You don't think I wouldn't have friends send me pictures of what happened in the St Moritz?" She shook her head and looked weary with disappointment when she said, "Do you know how many of those feathery little fuckers died tonight?"

Kitty seemed to consider this and then sniffed her disdain. "You've got your money," she said eventually. "Why would you care about how I got it?"

"I don't care," Jodie admitted. "But I won't tolerate the hypocrisy of you pretending you give a toss about those shitty fucking birds when you're perfectly happy to put them in the firing line when it suits your greedy, material ends."

"Perhaps you're right," Kitty said eventually. She glared at Jodie and spoke with venom when she said, "Some of my birds almost died this morning when they were killing your father."

Jodie nodded. She looked neither surprised nor particularly upset.

"I knew you were responsible for what happened to him."

"No," Kitty said quietly. "I'd say it was karma that was responsible for his death. My chicks just helped things along."

"No," Jodie said flatly. "You were responsible and I won't forget that."

"Is that a threat?" Kitty asked.

Jodie shook her head. "In a way you did me a favour. His estate now goes to me. You made me a wealthy woman this morning. I no longer need to run these hobo fights or even run this poxy-fucking-doss house. Thanks to you, I'm a rich woman with substantial resources."

"Does that mean you'll give me back my Bill?"

Jodie shook her head. "Not tonight."

Kitty's expression changed to one of outrage.

Jodie silenced her before she could say anything. "I'm running my final hobo fight tomorrow night," she explained. "If Bill wins, you can have him back."

"And if he loses?" Kitty asked doubtfully.

Jodie's smile was grim with self-satisfaction. "If he loses, I might give you your twenty grand back."

Raging Bill

The chef brought him a hamburger that looked relatively edible. The chef was a skinny-looking guy with sunken eyes whose gaze flashed repeatedly toward the strip of leather still tied to the roof beam above Dave's head. He introduced himself as Deacon and was then told to shut up by the woman who Dave recognised as Annabelle. Annabelle was wearing her usual uniform of combat gear and military boots. Armed with a taser which she kept pointed at him, she looked as though she had stepped from the pages of a teenage boy's fantasy comic about lesbian soldiers. Dave considered sharing this thought with her and then decided that it would not be wise to piss off a woman who already hated him and was now aiming a taser at his balls.

He nibbled gingerly at the burger, thinking that Deacon's culinary skills weren't worthy of the word 'chef', and then found himself wondering what credentials a person needed to become the private chef for kidnap victims. It crossed his mind that such a role could be given to a poisoner, a lunatic who foraged for food in bins, or even some pervert who had jacked off onto the finished burger and called the resulting concoction 'a splash of the chef's special sauce.' That thought was enough to kill his appetite and he dumped the half-eaten burger back onto the paper plate.

"Are you two both fighting tonight?" he called, wanting to break the silence of his own thoughts.

"We're not given a schedule," Bill said dourly. "An hour before the fight we're shackled, our fists are bound with bandages and barbwire, and then we're driven out to the deathmatch. The first thing we know about us being involved in a fight is when we have our door kicked open by Big Charlie and Annabelle."

Dave's bowels tightened. Whilst Bill's use of the word 'deathmatch' had been unsettling, for the first time, Dave fully understood he was being held so he could be used as one of the participants in Jodie's lethal hobo fights. The idea made him worried that he might not survive what the night had in store.

"Is it tonight when the next fight is happening?" he asked doubtfully.

"Wednesday night is fight night," Bill said solemnly.

"And, I'd have thought they were going to put you up first," Fred called.

Even though the man was calling from a different room, Dave knew Fred was talking to him. He didn't like the confidence with which Fred made the declaration. "What makes you think it will be me?" he asked doubtfully.

"Jodie likes to put the fresh blood in early," Fred explained. "You'll look lean. You'll look like a challenger. And you'll be too uncertain of the rules to know whether or not it's a genuine deathmatch."

Dave swallowed. He supposed there was a lot of sense in what Fred was saying and that idea made him worry that he was facing a very grave danger.

"I was put out to fight on my first night here," Fred added.

"Me too," Bill admitted.

"And I reckon you'll be fighting one of us," Fred added quickly. "Because I think the Terminator is no longer part of the equation."

It took Bill a moment to remember that there was a fourth fighter in the cells who had been given the nickname Terminator. He didn't recall hearing the man contribute to one of their shouted conversations since he'd been brought into the cells beneath the Majestic Hotel. "What do you reckon has happened to the Terminator?" Bill asked.

"I wouldn't like to hazard a guess," Fred admitted. "But we haven't heard from him all day so I'm thinking he went the same way as Dave's former cell holder."

"What happened to my former cell holder?" Dave asked, not sure he wanted an answer.

"Squid Game hanged himself last night," Bill explained. "That happens a lot around here. You'd be surprised by how many fighters don't make it to their first deathmatch."

Given the depressing trend of the conversation, Dave lay on his single bed and tried to clear his mind of all the negative thoughts that were now blackening his mood. He was hungry because he didn't want to eat spunk-sautéed burgers. He was the prisoner of a vicious sociopath who organised hobo deathmatches. He was most likely going to be involved in a violent and brutal fight this evening. And, unless things went in a direction that defied all common sense and logic, he was going to end up killing someone or being killed before he saw his next sunrise.

"You alright in there, Dave?" Bill called.

"Just trying to get some sleep," Dave told him.

"Good idea," Fred assured him. "Brooding on this shit is only going to send you on a downward spiral, and none of us want that."

Dave was nodding agreement, not bothering to reply for fear that someone might hear the threat of tears that would undoubtedly colour his voice. After breathing deeply and finally getting control of his emotions, Dave called, "Fred?"

"Yeah?"

"If we get you out of here, will you go back to your family?"

Fred laughed. "That's an easy promise to make because I know it's not going to happen. It's on the same level of likelihood as, if I win the lottery, I'll give you half the money."

"But will you?" Dave pressed. The point seemed stupidly important, and he needed to hear a response that offered some level of hope. He could feel himself clinging to this idea the way he had clung to the superstitious notion of solving Fred's case in the first place. He was suddenly stung by the importance of knowing, if Fred promised to return to his family in Sheffield if the chance arose, then perhaps there might be a hope of these dark events turning out for the best. "Will you?" Dave asked again. "Will you go back to your family if we get you out of here?"

"Sure I will," Fred agreed. The words sounded hollow, as though they were being used as a platitude. "Get me out of here, and I'll go back to my family."

"Promise?"

"I promise," Fred told him. There was suggestion of dark mirth in his voice as he added, "Going back to the family can't be much worse than where I've currently found myself."

Dave nodded and closed his eyes. Perhaps Fred was only saying the words to bring the conversation to a close, but he had promised which meant Dave had done as much as he could to meet the demands of his client. He kept his eyes closed, willed all the negative thoughts from his mind, and slowly drifted to sleep.

He was woken later when he found Deacon and a burly black man standing over him. Annabelle stood in the doorway of his cell, still holding the taser and glaring as though she was desperate for an excuse to use the damned thing. Deacon and Big Charlie put Dave's hands behind his back and then secured his wrists with a pair of cuffs.

"Take off his shirt," Annabelle snapped.

"Unfasten my wrists and I can take off my own shirt," Dave told her.

His comments were ignored. Big Charlie produced a blade and snatched a fistful of Dave's shirt. "Don't struggle," Big Charlie growled. "We don't want any mistakes, do we?"

"Unfasten my wrists and I can take off my own shirt," Dave repeated.

Big Charlie cut through the front of the shirt exposing Dave's pale chest. Because Dave's hands were fixed tight behind his back, he could do nothing when Big Charlie twisted him around and cut through the back of the shirt. The two halves pooled around Dave's wrists and were then cut away by Deacon who was armed with a pair of scissors.

"Are they taking your shirt off?" Fred called.

Dave didn't answer.

"They do that because Big Charlie has a thing about looking at man-titties," Fred explained and then laughed as though he had made the most uproarious remark.

Dave found himself staring at Big Charlie and knew the removal of his shirt had nothing to do with the man's desires to see exposed man-titties. Dave knew he was now shirtless because fights between bare-chested hobos would make for a more visually arresting spectacle.

"What are the man-titties like, Big Charlie?" Fred called, still laughing at his own overdeveloped sense of humour. "I mean, they're bound to be better than Annabelle's aren't they?"

"Shut the fuck up," Big Charlie said simply. "If I have to come in there to make you go quiet, they won't be calling you Freddie Four-Fingers when I come out of your cell."

Dave tried not to think what threat was implied by Big Charlie's words but he noted it was sufficiently menacing to make Freddie fall silent. He was pushed face first onto the single bed and he heard Annabelle giving instructions to Deacon.

"Get his hands into fists," she insisted. "Then bandage them."

"Why am I bandaging them?" Deacon asked.

"Because we'll be wrapping his fists with barbwire and, if his hands are bandaged, he'll be more likely to use them as weapons."

Dave considered resisting and not making his hands into fists but it was easier to comply rather than run the risk of Deacon's clumsiness or Annabelle's anger. The bandage was being tied in tightening loops around his clenched fist until it felt as though his hands were inside balls of fabric the size of balloons. Then he felt the barbwire being wrapped around his hands in rigid, tight rings.

"He'll do," said Annabelle. "Leave him there. We'll get the other one done now."

And then Dave was alone, still face down on the bed, with his hands bandaged and cuffed behind his back and the humiliating sensation creeping through his thoughts that the night was only going to get worse.

"What happens if I need to pee?" he called.

"If you need to pee, just piss yourself," Annabelle called back. "That won't be the worst thing to happen to you this evening."

His hands were still secured behind his back when he was dragged from his cell and encouraged up the rickety wooden stairs that led from the cellar. He was marched through the kitchen to the back door of the Majestic Hotel and bundled out into the night where the open rear doors of a Transit van awaited him.

Big Charlie lifted him into the vehicle and Dave found himself sitting on the floor, secured to one of the panels, facing a similarly secured man with a grisly beard, a bare chest and identical bandages and bindings to Dave. It did not take a great stretch of his powers as a private investigator to guess that this man was Raging Bill. Lowering his voice to a whisper, fearful the driver and those in the front might overhear if he spoke too loudly, Dave said, "Do you think we can both make a break for it?"

"A break?" Bill asked doubtfully.

"The plan I was talking about the other night," Dave prompted. "One of us gets thrown into the audience and the other runs into the sea and escapes by swimming up to the nearest pier. If that chance occurs, are you going to make a break for it?"

Bill shook his head sadly. "I'm sorry, man," he said quietly. "But when we start to fight, I'm going to be going at it for all I'm worth. It's a fight to the death and I'm not going to let my guard down until I'm either defeated or I'm the last one standing."

"But together-" Dave started.

He got no further.

"I'm giving you fair warning," Bill said. "Once they've taken our cuffs off, I won't be pulling any punches and I've got no intention of losing. Once they've taken off our cuffs, I'm going to fight you and, if I'm able, I'm going to kill you."

Birds of a Feather

Deacon locked the kitchen door after Annabelle, Jodie and Big Charlie had departed in the Transit. It was a little after midnight and he suspected he had an hour to put his plan into action. Any time over that was not guaranteed.

The world outside the kitchen was nothing more than night-blackened windows that had been transformed into obsidian mirrors which reflected his own miserable features. Deacon poured himself a big glass of scotch from the bottle that Jodie kept in the back of the kitchen cabinet and downed it in one. It was a cheap blend, and the liquid was fire at the back of his throat, but it helped steel his nerves for what was needed.

For the past few days he had been coming to the decision that he had to make amends for the error of his ways. He had sold a woman into slavery and put her in a situation where she had to kill or be killed. It was a horrific thing to have done to another human being and Deacon was determined to make amends.

Consequently, he had decided that tonight was the night when he was going to put things right.

The male fighters were usually held in the now-empty rooms of the basement. Deacon had fed each of them over the past few days and even been part of the team that led the fighters, one by one, to their scheduled bathroom breaks.

The female fighters were still secured in the attic and, after working there for a few days, Deacon now felt sufficiently familiar with the layout that he could try to facilitate their escape. He had cooked for all four women. He had been one of the two guards who escorted each of them from their cell on scheduled toilet breaks. And he knew, if anyone could help those women escape, it would be him.

The Majestic Hotel wasn't currently running to capacity: only twenty of its sixty rooms were occupied. This meant, whilst the hotel wasn't empty, there weren't an abundant amount of service-users roaming the corridors and potentially interrupting his plans to free the imprisoned female fighters.

The thought of what he was planning sent a shiver of trepidation tickling down his spine and Deacon had to have another stiff scotch before he'd gained enough Dutch courage to leave the kitchen to start making some form of reparation. He walked slowly to the upper floor of the Majestic, unsettled by the sounds of the quiet hotel. There were sounds of sleep and snores coming from behind some doors. He could have sworn he heard someone fapping behind another door and he hurried on, sure that he didn't want to hear that. His life had sunk to a low point where he was selling young women into the violent slavery of fighting in deathmatches and then working as a chef for kidnap victims. He had sunk to the point where he was desecrating corpses and helping bury them in the sand. He didn't want it to sink to the point where he was listening to hobos whacking off.

On the third floor of the Majestic, behind a locked door that faced the lift, lay the stairs to the attic. Deacon unfastened the door with one of the keys on the chatelaine he had taken from Jodie and slowly began the ascent.

During the days when this building had belonged to a large Edwardian family, the attic rooms were the sleeping quarters of maids and servants. They had been small, claustrophobic, designed with little ventilation, and existed with no thought for the comfort of the occupant. They remained less appealing now, Deacon thought, as he opened the door to the first room and found a miserable-looking woman glaring at him.

She was a skinny blonde with large boobs and long legs. She was sprawled on a single bed, identical to all the others in the cells, and was wearing an oversized man's plaid shirt for warmth and to cover her modesty.

"What do you want, Chef?" Her tone was sharp and sceptical, as though she already knew why she, a female prisoner, had a male visitor at this late hour of the night. "Have you come here to get some action? Does the Little Chef want to hide his little sausage?"

"I want to get you out of here," Deacon said quickly.

Her frown was suspicious. "Why?"

"Because it's not right you being here," he snapped. "I'm freeing all of you, so just hurry up and get yourself out of here before they get back."

She blinked at him, her expression somewhere between sceptical and incredulous. He saw her start to slide from the bed but he was already moving onto the next cell and opening the door for that prisoner.

The occupant for this cell was a brunette. Like her neighbour, she wore an oversized man's plaid shirt, and was laid indolently on a single bed. Unlike the blonde, it seemed the brunette knew what was happening because she'd clearly been listening to his conversation. She fixed him with an expression of cold pity as she said, "Jodie will have you killed for letting us go." She held up a finger and then said, "No. I think you'll be lucky if she just kills you."

Deacon figured she was right. He saw no reason to argue the point. "Get yourself down the stairs," he told the brunette. "If you act quickly, you should be able to get out of the front door and make your escape."

"And where do I go from there?" the brunette asked.

Deacon shrugged. "Go wherever you think you'll be safe," he said dismissively. Then he was stepping away and going to the next door.

His plan had gone as far as unlocking these doors and setting the female prisoners free. He didn't know what they were going to do once they were away from the Majestic Hotel, and he wasn't sure he cared. His conscience would be appeased by the act of giving them freedom and that was as much as he felt he needed for the moment.

It took two attempts to find the right key before the third door swung open. He found himself staring at Cheryl and she looked distinctly unhappy. Like her fellow inmates, she was wearing the uniform of an outsized plaid shirt and nothing else. Her legs were still marked by the cuts and scars of her last fight. Her face was darkened by the purple and yellowy-grey of fading bruises. When she saw it was Deacon standing at the door, her scowl transformed into a sneer of contempt.

"What the fuck are you doing here?"

"I'm setting you free."

"I ought to fucking murder you," Cheryl muttered.

Deacon nodded agreement. "That's the least I deserve," he admitted. "But, before you do that, will you let me unlock the door for this final cell?" He didn't wait for her to reply. Instead, he turned to find the fourth door and realised the way was blocked by the brunette and the blonde who he had already released. "Why haven't you guys left yet?" he demanded.

"We've got nowhere to go," the blonde told him.

"And we figured we'd be safer together," the brunette added.

"Well, whether it's alone or together, you've got to get out of here," Deacon insisted. "Jodie and her entourage will be back in less than an hour and hell's going to break loose when they come up here and find you're no longer in your cells." He pushed between the blonde and the brunette and opened the fourth door. There was another blonde in this room, her body ravaged with scars that suggested she had been in one of the more recent fights.

"You're free to go," Deacon told her. "But you have to hurry up."

Cheryl slammed a fist into the back of his head. The blow was unexpected and hard enough to drive him face-first into the wall of the final cell. The world turned momentarily black and stars erupted in the periphery of his vision. He staggered for a moment, lost his balance and then stumbled to the floor. As he ebbed close to losing consciousness, Deacon figured he deserved such a brutal assault and possibly worse.

"What the fuck are you playing at?" Cheryl demanded.

He pulled himself from the floor and glared at her. "I'm setting you guys free," he explained. "I thought I'd mentioned as much. We've got a small window of opportunity here. Jodie, Charlie and Annabelle are all out with one of the fights and–"

Cheryl punched him again. This blow hit him in the face and he felt a tooth being loosened. He could understand why she had been so successful in her own deathmatch. Cheryl clearly knew how to handle herself in a confrontation and each punch she delivered struck its target and left him staggering.

"Why?" Cheryl demanded.

"What do you mean?" he barked. "This is the right thing to do, isn't it?"

"If it's the right thing to do, why are *you* doing it?"

The brunette placed a hand on Cheryl's arm. "What's your grudge against this guy?"

"This is the bastard that sold me into this fighting," Cheryl said, twisting her arm free. "I trust him as far as I can throw the fucker." She pulled herself from the brunette's clutches and smashed another punch into Deacon's face. This one broke his nose and had him staggering back until he found himself sitting on the bed of cell four. He cupped a hand over his injured face, trying to staunch the blood flow and reminding himself that he deserved every twinge of this pain and then more.

"I'm trying to make amends," he said as he struggled to stand up. "For God's sake, Cheryl," he muttered. "I can understand you wanting to hurt me. I deserve your anger and your violence and everything else you want to throw at me. But I really think you need to get out of here whilst you have the chance."

"He's got a point," one of the blondes agreed. She was glancing anxiously around the empty room and then casting her gaze toward the end of the corridor where the stairs descended into the rest of the Majestic Hotel. "They could be back at any moment."

"OK," Cheryl agreed. She jabbed a finger at Deacon's chest and said, "You're going to take the four of us back to your place. You're going to give us money, lodging and food and you'll supply us with a base of operations as well."

"A base of operations? What for?"

"What for?" Cheryl echoed. She grinned wickedly and said, "We need a base of operations because we're going to have our revenge."

Fight or Flight

The promenade at North Shore was layered into different levels. The highest point was where the tableaux illuminations sat, their flashing and flickering images shining east toward the trams, traffic and tourists that dawdled past, bathed in bright and colourful lights. Moving west, going behind the tableaux, was like stepping backstage at a theatre. The glamour and glitz were gone. The world became dark and the land slipped away to a narrow cycle lane and a handful of dog-walking paths that were littered with forgotten beer cans and uncollected turds.

Kitty picked her way through the detritus of the dog paths and continued west, heading along one of the abrupt walkways that lead sharply down from the clifftops to the concrete sea defences one hundred feet below. The area was unlit, blacker than murder, and should have been unoccupied.

Except, she could see a circle of protected tiki torches, fluttering like an alien landing pad in the darkness of the beach. She allowed her eyes to adjust to the gloom, drinking in the scent of the briny air, feeling the night's chill raise goosebumps on her bare arms, and listening to the incessant hiss of the faraway sea. The night was so dark she could almost feel it pressing against her like a weight.

"Come to me, my chicks," she muttered.

In one hand she clutched the silver gull. Whatever energy channelled through the trinket was enough to bring a silent flock whispering down to join her on the sea defences. They were creatures that brought comfort because she knew, as long as the gulls were nearby, she would never come to any harm. They were her guardians and, as long as she held the silver gull, her guardians would always be there to protect Kitty and those she loved.

As her eyes adjusted she saw, in the centre of the circle of tiki torches, two grizzled-looking figures facing off against each other. She recognised Bill immediately with his full-length beard and straggly hair. He was marked with a big black X sprayed across his chest and his back. She could see a few more ribs than she was used to observing and she worried that, during his imprisonment, he'd been mistreated, abused and underfed. That idea made her resolve harden and she was determined to exact revenge this evening.

Bill's opponent, looking younger and not quite so careworn as her lover, had a large letter O sprayed on his back and his front. This man had the physique of someone who might not have been in peak physical fitness: but he was certainly not out of condition. His biceps looked firm. His build looked wiry, and his posture struck her as belonging to a confident and capable man. Kitty thought, if she'd been asked to bet on which man would win the fight, her money would have been on Bill's opponent. It was a thought that made her feel worried for her partner and traitorous for the lack of faith she was showing him.

Both men had bandaged fists that were bound tightly with barbwire. Even from this distance, Kitty could see that they both looked ready to kill. Given the way that Jodie was encouraging the audience into a state of death-lust with prompts and agitations, Kitty was not surprised that her heartbeat quickened with anxiety. She heard phrases like 'fight to the death' and 'there will be blood.' She felt lightheaded at the thought of her Bill being involved in something so dangerous.

"We have to get closer," Kitty told her flock.

The flutter of wings behind her told Kitty that her flock were following her lead. She started down the slippery steps that led from the sea defences to the beach. It was late and dark and she knew, if she took one wrong step, the unforgiving stone would snatch her down and smash her brittle bones. If she fell, the only options available would be to lay on the beach until the tide came in and drowned her, or shout for help from Jodie and her brutal friends. Of those two choices, she figured drowning would probably be the safest and most pain-free option. If Jodie caught her broken on the beach, Kitty knew she would suffer at the woman's hands. Nevertheless, braving every step of the danger, she gripped tight onto the rusted metal banister and shuffled as swiftly down the stairs as her elderly bones could manage.

"Marked with the letter X," she heard Jodie call. "We have our undefeated champion: Raging Bill."

The words floated across the empty sand with surprising clarity. Kitty could hear the distance in each syllable but that didn't stop her from understanding every word. More than ever before, she despised Jodie Crawford and wanted to see the woman get the comeuppance that she so truly deserved. Jodie had kidnapped Bill and so many other men and women. She'd been responsible for murders and death and untold suffering. The idea of giving the woman a taste of her own medicine was enough to make a smile of bitter anticipation spread over Kitty's lips as she stepped off the last of the stone stairs and found herself standing on the sand.

"And," Jodie continued, oblivious to the fact that her voice was carrying to a woman who despised her with a passion that went beyond anything she'd ever known. "Marked with the letter O – new to the circuit and clearly here to make an impression – we have the phenomenal fighter that is Dangerous Dave."

Kitty didn't like that name. Her Bill should not have to face someone with a name that sounded as violent as 'Dangerous Dave'. She gestured for her flock to continue following and started hurrying toward the lights of the tiki torches.

"I'll be taking bets over the next five minutes," Jodie told her audience. "And keep in mind this is a deathmatch, so the result is never going to be in dispute."

Kitty felt ill at the idea of her Bill being involved in such a violent interaction and her thoughts raced at a way to try and find a way to resolve the situation. She didn't want to send in a flock of gulls just yet because she feared Jodie and her thugs would just take their fighters and flee from the beach before Kitty could help Bill to escape.

It made more sense to wait until everyone was invested with the fight, and then take action. She clutched the silver gull in her hand more tightly and slowed her approach, fearful she would be seen by those at the periphery of the torchlight.

A large black man sat behind the wheel of a Transit van that was parked on the sand. Beside him, in the passenger seat of the van, Kitty could see a butch-looking woman who was smoking a hand-rolled cigarette. Now that she was closer to the tiki torches, she could make out a crowd of maybe two dozen gamblers. These numbers were enhanced by Jodie's guards, some of whom were walking through the audience whilst others stood just outside the circle of tiki torches training tasers on Dave and Bill.

Kitty studied the site and tried to work out the best way to prepare an attack. She didn't consider herself a great tactician, but she did think she could see how best to play this game.

The audience for the fight were the least protected. Kitty could send a small flock of gulls to pick off the audience and they would fall like dominoes. But, as entertaining as that attack might prove, Kitty knew it wouldn't help Bill to escape his predicament or avoid the wrath of his captors.

Her gut made her want to attack Jodie and have the bitch pecked to death, but Kitty didn't think that was practical. She knew her birds would be able to murder the woman in mere seconds, but Jodie's taser-wielding henchmen would ensure that Bill and Dangerous Dave were bundled back into the waiting Transit van and from there, Kitty would be left trying to negotiate her partner's release through a team without a leader. That was not an option worth considering because she worried that a new leader might think it safest to destroy any evidence of what had been happening, and that could mean Bill's existence was placed in jeopardy.

Which was why she decided the taser-wielders were going to be the target of her first phase of attack. Once they were taken out of the equation, Kitty was going to send a couple of birds to attack members of the audience and start a small panic. She would use that distraction to call to Bill and have him extricated from the fight and then the pair of them would escape across the beach. To cover their exit, Kitty intended to send whatever birds were remaining in a full assault on Jodie Crawford. Those members of Jodie's staff who remained would be torn between their duties to ensure Bill remained a captive and to keep Jodie safe, and she figured that they would all opt for that final choice.

She drew a steadying breath, took a step closer to the scene of the deathmatch and waited for the fight to begin.

"Tonight's competitors are local boy, Raging Bill: undefeated winner of the last ten matches…" Jodie paused for a moment, allowing a handful of audience members to applaud and shout encouragement. "And he'll be fighting against our esteemed visitor, Dangerous Dave."

The cheers for Dangerous Dave were loud but, Kitty figured the smart money was against him. No one got to be undefeated champion over ten matches without having some serious fighting skills. Although he had a scary name and a suggestion of youthfulness on his side, Kitty could see the man had a potbelly hanging over the waistband of his jeans and he didn't have the same expression of determination that her Bill wore.

"Please remember," Jodie told her audience. "These two hobos are going to fight each other to the death. The winner will be the last one standing."

"To the death!" the audience chanted with bloodthirsty excitement. "To the death!"

Jodie nodded and stepped out of the ring. "To the death!" she called loudly.

And as those words echoed across the beach, the hobo fight began.

Dangerous Dave did not look like a man who wanted to participate in violence and was backing away as Bill approached him. He had his hands raised defensively, and he dodged and ducked as Bill threw barbwire punches toward his face and chest.

"Stop running away," someone called.

"Stand your ground and fight, you yellow bastard," yelled another.

Kitty was wanting to shout something similar because she had decided that she would send her birds to make their initial attack when the first proper blow connected. She figured that would be the point of absolute distraction, when Jodie's staff were most invested in the fight and the audience were watching to see how badly the first injury had proved. She watched Bill step closer to Dave, jabbing and punching, and she watched Dave take steps backwards as he managed to avoid every blow intended for him.

"Hit the fucker," someone in the audience yelled. "Take his fucking head off."

"Kill the chickenshit bastard."

"Stand still," Kitty whispered.

Bill feinted a jab with his left and then stepped in to deliver a powerhouse slam from his right fist. This caught Dave hard in the gut and was heavy enough to lift him from his feet. Dave doubled over and screamed and then fell to the floor as the audience cheered.

"Now," Kitty told her flock.

The birds responded as though they'd read her mind. Six swooped down from the sky, dividing into pairs at the last moment with each pair taking on one of the guards that was wielding a taser. Kitty didn't bother to watch and see how effective the attacks were: she trusted her gulls and knew they were formidable enemies. The screams and cries of the guards were enough to tell Kitty that her plans were working successfully. Those cries seemed to have been amplified over the stunned silence of everyone who was watching the unexpected attack.

"Second phase," Kitty commanded.

Six more birds took to the air and threw themselves down on random audience members. The attacks were harsh and vigorous and the small crowd that had circled the tiki torches was instantly dispersed as individuals ducked down, hurled protective hands over their heads, and started running blindly into the darkness.

Kitty was watching Jodie and could see the woman already understood what was going on. Jodie knew about Kitty's control of the birds and she understood that this power might be used against her. Jodie was shouting commands to her generals as she ducked from imagined attacks from the sky. Kitty heard her shout, "Get those two back in the van."

And that was when Kitty gave the final command to the remainder of her flock. "Attack the bitch," Kitty screamed.

The remaining birds understood the instruction and acted immediately. Kitty wasn't sure how many of them were flying but she briefly lost sight of the tiki torch circle as a darkness of birds swept through the sky and descended on Jodie. The attack would have been immediately devastating if Jodie had not snatched a tiki torch from the sand and used it to swipe at the sky and beat the birds away from her as she retreated back to the van.

"You saved me," Bill said, appearing at Kitty's side.

"You're not saved yet," Kitty told him. "We need to get off this beach and back on shore, to safety."

"You saved me," Bill said again. "Thank you."

And then he was urging her to run at his side through the night as the cries of gulls and their victims rang across the beach. Kitty dared to risk a backward glance over her shoulder and was infuriated to see Jodie climbing into the rear of the Transit whilst two of her employees dragged the unconscious body of Dangerous Dave behind her. There were a couple of dead figures on the beach and a handful of seagull corpses. And, whilst that meant the exercise was neither a defeat nor a victory, Kitty took solace from the fact that she had managed to help her beloved Bill to escape.

Fight like a Girl

For Dave, it was the longest and most miserable week of his life.

Jodie was cursing the name of Kitty Wakes as the Transit sped them from the beach and back to the Majestic. She was still growling threats for how she was going to have the woman punished when they got back to hotel, and then she discovered that Deacon was no longer there.

Dave had caught a vicious hook from Bill. Because the bastard was wearing a barbwire glove, decorated with a razor blade, that meant the air had not just been pushed out of Dave's lungs: Bill had also managed to score a handful of penetrating wounds. Dave was bleeding from a deep slice to his stomach and had become unsettled by the worry that the barbwire might have penetrated the delicate tubing of his small intestines. If that happened he knew the risk of sepsis, blood poisoning and death were seriously increased. However, his injuries were considered of negligible importance compared to the suffering that had been inflicted on Jodie when a couple of birds had pecked at her face and torn a small strip of flesh from under her eyelid.

Jodie screamed in discomfort from her injuries and made it clear to anyone within earshot that she was going to have her revenge. Each time she spoke about this, Jodie made it known that nothing was more important than the assurance of her safety and the fact that she should be kept from suffering any repercussions for the hobo fights.

Big Charlie had been asking what she wanted them to do about the tiki torches, audience, tasers and staff that were still at the scene of the fight and Jodie told him he would be returning there after an hour to clean up any mess. They were still having this conversation when they returned to the Majestic Hotel, and this was how Jodie came to discover that Deacon had disappeared.

"Tell Deacon to go with you," Jodie told Annabelle and Big Charlie. "He can help with the clean-up."

"Where is he?" asked Annabelle.

Jodie rolled her eyes. "How the fuck should I know where he is?" she demanded. "I've been out with you two tossers all evening." She was putting disinfectant on the wound beneath her eye, trying to kill any germs before they could cause a problem, and clearly suffering from worse pain with this cure than she'd suffered with the seagull attack. "Check his bedroom. Check the attic. Just find the fucker and tell him he's going with you."

That was the last Dave saw of the exchange before he was bundled down the stairs and thrust unceremoniously into his cell. The room was as small and unwelcoming as he remembered. He collapsed miserably on the bed, curled into a foetal position to try and ease the pain on his stomach.

"What happened?" called Fred.

"Bill escaped," Dave called back. "There was a mad seagull attack. It was like something out of *Birdemic*, but with better special effects."

The momentary silence that followed this comment made Dave feel sure that Fred had never seen *Birdemic*. "Good for Bill," Fred said cheerfully.

Dave looked at the still-bleeding scars on his stomach and shook his head with bitter disappointment. "Yeah," he said stiffly. "Good for Bill."

Wherever the conversation could have gone from that point was immediately discounted when they both heard Jodie's outraged roar of frustration coming from the kitchen above them.

"All of them?" she demanded. Her voice was close to a screech with the absolute fury in her tone. "Every one of them has gone?"

Neither Dave nor Fred could hear the reply.

"Get yourself back out there now," Jodie shrieked. "I want you cleaning up on the beach and then I want you finding Deacon and those four bitches. Do you understand me?"

"What's going on?" Fred called.

"It sounds like Deacon has done a runner with the female fighters," Dave explained, unable to say the words without smiling. "I didn't think that he had the balls to do something so brave." He thought about it for a moment longer and then found himself laughing delightedly at this outcome.

He wouldn't have been laughing if he had known that this development would have such a negative impact on his own situation. Without Deacon the cooking responsibilities fell to Annabelle and Big Charlie. Big Charlie's idea of culinary expertise was a toasted cheese sandwich and Annabelle could just about open a tin of soup and heat the contents in a microwave. Between them they produced meals that were unappetising, unsatisfying and, given the state of the bowls they were served in, worryingly unhygienic.

Dave kept a wary eye on the injuries he had sustained and was relieved that the cuts seemed to heal, reddened only a little bit, before subsiding to itchy scars. He and Fred kept a constant ear open to hear more of Jodie's exclamations but there was nothing forthcoming. Even when they asked Big Charlie and Annabelle what was happening when the pair served their meals, neither of the guards offered any chance to discuss what had caused Jodie to be so furious with Deacon.

"You'll be fighting next Wednesday," Annabelle told Dave. "And Jodie's organised for a Northumberland contender to come down here and beat the shit out of you."

"Who's the contender?" Dave asked.

"Some guy they're calling Hadrian the Wall."

Dave considered this name and decided the organisers of the Northumberland hobo fights were just as lacking in creativity and imagination as Jodie. He didn't bother voicing the opinion, sure it would be enough to earn him a beating.

"Is he any good?"

"Twenty confirmed kills," Annabelle said gleefully. "And I expect it will be twenty-one after Friday night. The guy's built like a brick shithouse and he doesn't hold back."

Dave kept his face fixed into an insouciant grin. He didn't want Annabelle to see that her words were causing him any concern. He was still grinning when she'd left him alone in his cell so he could have a shouted conversation with Fred. Annabelle had continued to taunt him with similar comments each day when she and Big Charlie delivered his meals. By the time a week had elapsed Dave felt it very likely he was going to die at the hands of the Northumberland fighter.

Those thoughts were almost crushing him when Annabelle and Big Charlie took him out in the Transit to face his competitor.

Hadrian wasn't big, as Annabelle had described him: he was fucking enormous. Dave didn't think he'd seen a guy who was seven foot tall before. Hadrian climbed out of the van, stretching shoulder muscles that looked like canon-balls and flexing biceps the size of footballs.

"I'm going to fucking die," Dave muttered.

"I won't be betting on you," Annabelle agreed.

Then she was snatching Dave out of the van and dragging him into the centre of the tiki torch ring. Jodie was already there and extolling Dave's virtues with a cheerful enthusiasm that belied the seriousness of his situation.

"This is Dangerous Dave facing the Northumberland Goliath," Jodie called cheerfully. "And you all know how the original David and Goliath fight turned out, so I'm thinking this guy might be worth a punt."

The silence that followed this suggestion was enough for Dave to know that there would be no money being placed on him this evening. He didn't blame anyone for identifying him as the potential loser. He had already decided that was the most likely outcome for the evening.

Jodie told the audience that the fight would begin in five minutes and then went through the process of taking bets and offering a range of odds to anyone who cared to ask.

"I've got a bet with Big Charlie," Annabelle told Dave. There was a sneer of condescension in her tone. "I reckon you'll be dead within the first minute," she told him.

Dave considered taking a swing at her. His fists were already bandaged and bound with barbwire. No matter how swiftly he acted, Dave didn't think he'd be able to kill Annabelle. But he felt sure he could leave her permanently scarred. However, he would be instantaneously hit by two tasers and then expected to fight before his body had a chance to recover from that pain. That would mean Hadrian the Wall had even less opposition in the impending one-sided fight. But Dave figured it might be worth certain and inevitable death if he had a chance to inflict some retribution on Annabelle.

Then she'd stepped away from him and Dave realised he had no chance of striking her now. He cursed himself for missing the opportunity and stared miserably out into the blackness of the night beyond the tiki torches, wondering if there might be a chance for him to run into the darkness, swim out to the end of one of the piers, and wait there until the morning. He knew it was stupid to even entertain the idea. Jodie had heard him discussing this plan with Raging Bill and Freddie Four-Fingers so, even if he did manage to escape into the sea, the bitch would be waiting for him when he climbed onto the pier. And, after swimming through the freezing waters of the midnight Irish Sea, Dave figured he wouldn't be able to put up any fight. In short, the idea of managing any sort of escape seemed so far removed from reality that he figured it was more likely the seagulls would come and rescue him.

Jodie stepped into the illuminated circle and raised a hand. "Ladies and gentlemen," she called, turning 360° so that none of the audience felt excluded. "Thank you for coming to tonight's game. I trust you've all paid your admission fees and made suitable bets." She paused for a moment in case a member of the audience wanted to offer her more money or make an additional wager.

Dave's stomach tightened and he felt the unshakeable need to visit the lavatory. Whatever happened now, he knew it was going to hurt and he would likely be dead before morning. He didn't know what he'd done wrong with his life for it to come to such an unenviable position, and he wanted to argue that it wasn't fair.

"Tonight's competitors are local boy, Dangerous Dave: an undefeated champion..." Jodie paused for a moment, allowing a handful of audience members to applaud and shout encouragement. Dave figured, since his fight with Raging Bill hadn't resulted in his own death, he was technically undefeated. But he still thought Jodie was potentially misleading her audience with the claim.

"And Dangerous Dave will be fighting against our esteemed visitor from Northumberland this evening: Hadrian the Wall."

The cheers for Hadrian were loud, and it seemed clear to Dave that the smart money was on the man from Northumberland. Dave studied his opponent warily, his sharp eyes looking for some potential weakness he could exploit. In truth Hadrian was enormous, well-muscled and looked like he would be physically capable of tearing a man into small pieces. Dave figured this was the night he was going to meet his maker and he thought it would be Hadrian the Wall who sent him to that meeting.

"Please remember," Jodie told her audience. "These two gentlemen of the road are going to fight each other to the death."

Hadrian slammed his fists against the O on his chest. Because his hands were already wrapped in barbwire, the gesture made small rivulets of blood dribble from his pecs.

"I am so fucked," Dave thought miserably. "This guy is grinning whilst he beats himself in the tits. How badly is he going to hurt me?"

He didn't hear if Jodie said anything else. There was an abrupt cheer and then Jodie was stepping out of the ring and telling her audience, "To the death!"

The audience picked up her chant and called, "To the death!"

Dave swallowed, glanced up at the enormous figure bearing down on him and prepared to duck when the first blow was thrown in his direction. He managed to get his head down, hearing the whistle of air sweep just over his head, and for an instant he wondered if dodging that punch meant there was a chance for him to avoid being killed by his giant competitor.

Hadrian lifted one foot and kicked Dave in the chest.

Dave fell back onto the sand to a mixed response of cheers and groans. His chest was ringing with an explosion of pain – he felt certain he'd just lost a couple of ribs – and he understood that this was the night when he was finally going to die. It was not a depressing thought. He realised he'd managed to help several people with his P.I. work. He believed he had helped get Raging Bill free from the deathmatches and he only wished he had been able to reunite Freddie four-fingers with his family.

He was still thinking those thoughts when the sound of a thousand seagulls burst through the night and he heard the cries of shrieking and screaming fighters invading the tiki torch ring.

Seagulls from Hell

Deacon had been watching the setup of the fight, wondering why he had allowed himself to be drawn into this revenge scenario. Cheryl had pointed out to him that he owed her an enormous favour. When Deacon reminded her that he had been the one to free Cheryl from her imprisonment at the Majestic Hotel, Cheryl had tactfully observed that she wouldn't have needed to be released from her imprisonment if he hadn't sold her into slavery.

And it was obvious that Cheryl wanted revenge. She had insisted that her three fighting colleagues join them at the hobo deathmatch because she figured it would be the ideal moment to catch Jodie and her underlings at their most vulnerable. When the rumour-mill had told them that Jodie's prized fighter Raging Bill had escaped on the same night that she broke free, Cheryl told Deacon to find where Raging Bill was hiding so he too could be invited to watch Jodie suffering the fate she deserved. It surprised all of them that Raging Bill had asked to bring his frail wife along to the spectacle. Both Deacon and Cheryl suspected the woman had a mental disorder when she claimed to have some control over the seagulls.

Yet, whilst that claim sounded ludicrous, Deacon found himself changing his mind on the matter when Kitty sent the first of her seagulls attacking those around the tiki torches. She waited until the first punch was delivered, a powerful kick that knocked the weedier of the two fighters off his feet and onto his back. And then she sent in her flock of vicious, angry gulls.

The birds were ferociously obedient.

They flew out of the night sky and struck hard and fast against the guards wielding tasers. Deacon heard the birds making cawing sounds that were either angry or excited or simply the noises made by feathery killing machines as they launched themselves at their prey. There was the click and sizzle of a taser being accidentally fired and Deacon saw one of the audience members collapse to the floor, writhing sufficiently to take out one of the tiki torches.

"Phase two," Kitty commanded, pointing toward the torches.

At the same time as she said the words, Cheryl was leaping up, shrieking a piercing war cry, and running toward the fight. Her fists had been bound with bandages and then secured with barbwire. The same had been done for her three colleagues from the attic. Unlike when they had been fighting for Jodie, all three women were now dressed in jeans and sweatshirts. They followed the gulls as the birds rushed into the circle of tiki torches and started slamming their fists into anyone who stood in their way.

The audience were already running into the shadows, giving up on their bets and disappearing into the night. Whatever loyalty they felt for Jodie, or the fighter on whom they'd risked their money, it was nothing compared to the regard they had for their own safety. They ran shrieking and screaming, not caring which direction they took, so long as it put distance between themselves and the carnage that was occurring on the beach.

And Deacon had to admit it was carnage.

One of the taser guards had been blinded. He staggered on his knees, black streams of blood pouring from his empty eye sockets as he tried to catch his bearings. The other taser guard lay motionless beside the circle of tiki torches. Blood pumped from a wound at the side of his throat and Deacon figured, if the guy wasn't already dead, he wouldn't last much longer.

Hadrian, in the middle of this carnage, looked indecisive. It seemed obvious he wanted to destroy his opponent, but he also wanted to swipe at the flock of threatening birds that swept past him having interrupted his fight. Then three women were on him, each one beating his body with their barbwire fists, and Hadrian went down like he'd stood on a trapdoor.

The women attacking him beat him remorselessly.

Hadrian tried to swing out with a violent blow but he was no match for the two blondes and the brunette. He raised a hand to slam his fist against one of them and a barbwire punch caught him in the groin. It was a brutal shot that left him backpedalling away from the injury. And, because he wasn't used to being in a defensive position, it was easy for the three women to overpower him and beat him to the ground.

Bill walked over to Dave and helped him up from the floor.

"Sorry I left you last week," Bill said easily as Dave struggled to his feet.

Dave was shaking his head. "You had an escape route and you took it," he admitted. "I would have done the same."

Bill shook his head. "I don't think you would have left me behind," he said honestly. "But thanks for saying that so I don't feel so bad." Bill lurched past Dave and delivered a furious kick to one of the guards.

Dave glanced down and saw the man had been regaining consciousness and reaching for his taser. He glanced at another guard and saw that Cheryl had already slammed a barbwire fist into the side of his head, leaving him motionless beside his weapon.

"Are these seagulls trained?" Dave asked Bill.

"My wife controls them," Bill explained.

As they watched, a pair of the gulls flew at Jodie. She ducked away from one but the other managed to strike her full in the face with its bodyweight. There was a scream of outrage and then she was floundering on the floor, beating her arms senselessly into the air, and sobbing as a flock of gulls descended on her. Their beaks pecked at her clothes and face, merciless in the way they squawked and tried to strip any piece of soft flesh available.

Big Charlie had been trying to get into the Transit when Cheryl stepped in front of him. He raised his hands in surrender and she took the opportunity to slam a jab directly into his face. The blow was hard enough to flatten his nose and make a spurt of blood erupt from just above his eye. Cheryl hit him with a second punch, this one going slightly lower, and her barbwire fist caught Big Charlie in the throat. There was an obscene popping sound and then he was clutching at his neck, falling to his knees and dying as he drowned in his own blood.

"Get that bitch," Cheryl insisted, pointing at Annabelle.

Dave didn't know who the instruction was intended for, but he figured he could help as much as anyone else. He started toward Annabelle who was now wielding a tiki torch. He watched as she kept two of the female fighters at bay and inched closer to the sanctuary of the Transit van.

"Get her," Cheryl insisted.

Three seagulls flew at Annabelle.

Annabelle hit the first with the tiki torch but the second one flew straight at her face and drove its beak into her eye socket. There was a chilling scream that went up an octave when the third bird pushed at her face, slapped its webbed feet against her cheeks, and then began to peck at her forehead. Annabelle collapsed to her knees and, when she was down, the brunette came over and smashed a barbwire fist into the side of her head.

Annabelle fell dead to the beach.

Deacon took a moment to glance around and saw that the fight was finished. Jodie, Big Charlie and Annabelle were all dead. That discovery made him smile. He could see that Hadrian the Wall had been reduced to little more than a disfigured pulp of flesh quivering on the sand. Hadrian had been blinded and crippled by the female fighters and, judging by the amount of blood that was darkening the crotch of his pants, Deacon figured they'd taken out quite a few of their frustrations on the man who now lay squirming in the sand.

There were the bodies of the guards who had been wielding tasers. None of them had survived. The rest of the crowd had also disappeared into the night. Hadrian's handlers had clearly decided to cut their losses and gone with the audience. Looking round, Deacon did not think there could have been a better outcome to the evening. He was about to say as much when Cheryl approached him and slammed her barbwire fist into his throat.

His eyes opened wide.

He tried to snatch a surprised breath and realised his lungs were no longer working. And then he was falling to the beach, unable to take a final breath before he died.

Back to the Treadmill

Dave usually found the treadmill relaxing: but not today. It was early morning, a week after the last of the Punch and Jodie show fights had been lost, and he ached from all the abuse his body had recently taken. Worse, dragging his mood on a downward spiral, Dave did not feel as though he had achieved a successful resolution for any of the people he had recently worked with.

He increased the pace of the treadmill he was using and shifted from trying to run 10K in an hour to trying to achieve 11K. His heart pounded. He felt a little lightheaded from the extra exertion, and he knew he wouldn't achieve that goal. But the physical distraction stopped him from fretting about those things he couldn't change.

The town was currently awash with hundreds of police officers investigating the surprising number of bodies that had been found buried beneath the coast's shoreline. A couple of them, Jodie and Big Charlie, had washed up a week earlier. Their appearance had caused enough of a stir to make officers search the area and, so far, they had managed to exhume a dozen soggy corpses from the sea. The newspapers were making out that it was the start of a huge investigation that was going to bring down a criminal empire.

Dave felt fairly confident that the investigation would go no further than finding the rest of the bodies. He had a contact at the police headquarters and, if his name did appear in any conversations about these mysterious deaths, he would receive sufficient warning to take his suitcase of money from reclaiming the Pagani Huayra Roadster, and be able to start a new life somewhere out of the local constabulary's catchment area.

Dave's phone rang shrilly through his headphones. He lifted his wrist and read the caller ID on his Fitbit: UNKNOWN CALLER. In his line of work it was not uncommon to get calls from strangers and he tapped the button on the headphones answering the call and waiting for the caller to speak.

"I'm looking for a guy called Dave."

"You've found one," he acknowledged.

"You were looking for my brother, Fred," the voice explained. "Where the fuck is he?"

Dave placed his feet on the sides of the treadmill and allowed the rubber to spin freely between his spread legs. "I sent you my report a week ago," he said coolly. "I located Fred. I told him you were concerned for his wellbeing. And I asked him to contact you to give you some reassurance that he was fine and well." He paused, drew breath into his oxygen-starved lungs and added, "Didn't he do that?"

There was a moment's hesitation. "Yeah," the caller admitted. There was obvious reluctance in the voice. "He phoned up and said he wouldn't be coming home. But that's not what I wanted."

"Tough shit," Dave thought tiredly. "It's a better outcome than was going to happen." He kept those thoughts to himself as he stared out of the gym's plate-glass window and tried to wish the dark thoughts away.

"How much would it cost to have you bring him home to me?" the caller asked.

Dave considered his response for a moment and then ended the call. Reaching for his phone he put a block on the last number and then jumped back onto the treadmill, increasing the speed of the spinning rubber to 12K per hour, so his feet were pounding along at a lunatic pace that jolted his body with every step.

One of his fellow gym rats, a guy who preferred working with weights, had nodded at Dave on the treadmill and asked, half-jokingly, "What are you running from?"

Reflecting on the conversations with Fred's relative, Dave was beginning to think he might now know what he was running from, and he didn't think a treadmill would ever be enough to put distance between himself and all those things in the world that he so seriously despised.

A tramp stepped in front of him.

Dave recognised him as the man who had mocked his running earlier in the month. He figured there would be no point in making any comment on the man's poverty this time. Not only would that be unkind, but Dave figured the guy would have a comeback for such a putdown. As soon as he saw the sneer of derision on the man's dirty face, Dave closed his eyes and ran blindly. He didn't like running sightlessly into darkness but, sometimes, it was better to do that rather than see what was really happening in the world.

He thought that getting Bill and Kitty back together should have been a happy resolution to the week's events, but it wasn't. During the fight on the beach Kitty had lost some silver trinket she'd been carrying. Retrieving the damned thing was all the mad old bitch could talk about. She didn't seem to care about Bill. She didn't give a toss about any of those that had died or even any of those that had been saved: she only cared about that stupid lost trinket.

He opened his eyes and was not surprised to see that the mocking tramp had sauntered off, clearly unhappy that he wasn't getting the response he wanted. Outside the gym the street was early-morning empty, save for a pair of seagulls fighting over a discarded box that had once contained a burger and chips. The plate-glass was sufficiently robust to stop their cries from reaching his ears, but he could tell both creatures were agitated to the point of squawking death threats at each other.

That was when it happened.

He noticed Kitty walking miserably past the gym, her dirty-white coat wrapped tight around her bird-thin body as she hurried to visit Sainsbury's for some start-of-the-day necessities. He had been about to wave his hand at her in polite acknowledgement, even though he could see her lipless smile was turned down into a scowl of uncompromising fury. He watched her lurch into the road, her gaze fixed on the seagulls as she started to walk past them.

Curiously, both birds stopped fighting and turned to stare at her. Kitty stopped walking toward Sainsbury's and made a gesture at both creatures.

Dave was irritated to see she was standing in the middle of Cookson Street as she made this gesture, and he wondered what could be so important about waving at a seagull that it meant she wasn't getting out of the road and ensuring her own safety.

Kitty's gestures at the birds became more frantic.

The birds now seemed to be staring at her with an expression of thinly concealed hostility. Dave did not consider himself to be an expert in animal behaviour, but he thought it was easy enough to read the expressions on the faces of these soulless creatures: they were getting ready to attack.

Kitty made the gesture again. It was a snapping of her fingers and then a furious, almost maniacal pointing gesture that was fixed on both birds. She was clearly trying to evoke some response from the creatures but the response she did evoke wasn't likely the one she wanted.

The larger bird went for her face. The smaller one went lower, snapping at her hand and its sharp beak managed to slice through two fingers in a single bite.

Dave jumped off the treadmill, horrified by what he was seeing and wondering how he was meant to help. Kitty stepped away from the onslaught of the two birds, flapping her hands in front of her face and trying to strike at everything and anything that fluttered near her.

She stepped back into the path of a bus.

Dave rushed away from the treadmill to try and get outside but the gym was secure. To get out of the building he had to tap his access code into the keypad beside the doorway and, because his hands were trembling, he messed it up twice. By the time he had made it outside, and hurried alongside the gym to where Kitty had fallen, he felt sure it would be too late.

The bus was still parked there.

Kitty lay dead on the floor with a seagull pecking angrily at her cold face.

The driver had climbed out of the bus and was staring miserably at Kitty's motionless body. "She just stumbled back when they started attacking her," the driver explained. "I didn't have a chance to stop."

Dave knelt down beside the fallen body and felt for a pulse that wasn't there. He pushed his hand at the remaining bird that flapped at him, and it grudgingly flew back to its mate. "You'd best call the police," he told the driver. "It's a little late for an ambulance."

"She's dead," the driver gasped.

Dave nodded.

"Where do these fucking things come from?" the driver demanded. He was glaring at the pair of seagulls which had returned to their fight over the polystyrene burger box. "Where the fuck do they come from?"

Dave passed his hand over Kitty's face, closing her eyes so she was no longer staring at the world with an expression of pained surprise. He stood up, listening to his knees pop as he made the movement, and wondered if it would be worth telling the driver that Blackpool's resident birds were the seagulls from hell.

About the Author

Ashley Lister is a prolific writer of fiction, having written more than sixty full length novels and over a hundred short stories. Aside from regularly blogging about poetry and writing in general, Ashley also teaches creative writing. He lives in Lancashire, England.

www.ashleylister.com

Other titles from Ashley Lister:
Fearless: a dark tale from Innsmouth
Unearthed: a dark tale from Innsmouth
Cursed: a dark tale from Innsmouth
Kurgan: a dark tale from Innsmouth
Escape: a dark tale from Innsmouth
Dagon: a dark tale from Innsmouth

Conversations with Dead Serial Killers
Blackstone Towers
PayBack Week
Death by Fiction
Doll House
Raven & Skull

Old People Sex (and other highly offensive poems)

How to Write Short Stories and Get Them Published
How to Write Erotic Fiction and Sex Scenes

1

The thing that few people appreciated about Ed Gein was his skill as a seamstress. Clive had sat through every episode of the *Great British Sewing Bee* and, whilst the finalists on that show invariably produced some nice-looking creations in the last episode of each series, and sometimes that was when they were working with awkward fabrics such as organza, pleated lace or chiffon, none of them had (yet) been challenged with creating something original from human skin. To Clive's mind it was an injustice that everyone looked at Ed Gein's work (the belt made from nipples, the lampshade made from Mary Hogan's face, and the chairs, fully upholstered, in human skin) and all they saw was the *Grand Guignol* horror that came from murder, the desecration of graves, and the violation of corpses. No one appreciated the man for his craftsmanship and finesse with a needle and thread.

Clive sat back at his desk, surveying the screen that held his notes on Gein and wondering how close his latest book was to being ready for publication. There were hundreds of biographies covering Gein, describing him as the Plainfield Butcher, the Plainfield Ghoul and the Grandfather of Gore, and explaining how he had been the role model for fictional monsters such as Leatherface in *The Texas Chainsaw Massacre*, Norman Bates in Robert Bloch's *Psycho*, and even Buffalo Bill in *Silence of the Lambs*.

Clive's approach to the biography had been different. Rather than go on about the lawlessness and illegality of Gein's actions with the usual ghoulish voyeurism concerning murder, grave-robbing and skin-removal, Clive wanted to celebrate the Ed Gein that the history books had overlooked. Gein was a hard-working labourer. Gein was a loving son who aspired to be just like his mother. And Gein was a diligent researcher who had studied subjects as diverse as the Nazis, cannibalism and, if his well-thumbed copy of *Grey's Anatomy* was any indicator, human biology.

Not that Gein was the only subject of the biographies he had written. Clive had published one volume on the comforting bedside manner of Dr Harold Shipman foregrounding the under-reported benevolent side of the world's most prolific serial killer. He had also written about the forbidden romance between Ian Brady and Myra Hindley, and wanted to write about the passion that kept Fred and Rose West together. Importantly, and it was a consistent theme throughout all of the books he was writing, Clive wanted to talk about the fact that some of these 'notorious killers' had managed to grow up to appear like unassuming and normal adults despite the trauma of abusive childhoods. He knew they'd grown up to appear unassuming and normal because neighbours, witnesses and others involved in testifying against these people, always described them as being 'unassuming and normal.'

He supposed the project struck a personal chord for him because, if not for fate and circumstances, he figured he too could have been another name on the long list of serial killers who had been captured and punished by a society that didn't understand. He had been brought up by abusive parents. He had suffered a minor head trauma before reaching puberty and he had been a bedwetter until his mid-teens. He enjoyed lighting small fires and putting down rat traps and these were all indicators, on some liberal scale, that suggested he would have a propensity for being a serial killer. Crucially, he was a loner who enjoyed pornography and horror films and, whilst that described every kid he'd gone to school with, and every adult he'd met since, he knew this was also used as a standard yardstick for measuring the potentiality of serial killers.

His phone rang.

The caller-ID told him it was his brother, Derek.

Clive answered the phone before it had rung for a third time.

"Where are you?" Derek asked.

"I'm working on my writing," Clive said simply. "I was writing about Ed Gein. Do you know he had a lovely smile?"

"Is Gein the one who was making a bodysuit out of human flesh so he could look like his mother?"

"Don't say it like that. You make it sound weird."

Derek sighed. "There's a *Conversations with Dead Friends* tonight here at the Playhouse," he explained. He sounded as though he was speaking with forced patience. "You promised me you'd be here to assist with the hot readings and the after-show sales."

"I can help with the hot readings from here," Clive assured Derek. He sat in front of three flat screen monitors. One of them showed the latest draft of his Gein manuscript. The other two, respectively, showed some bondage porn he'd been perusing and the login page for the Thrill-Kill website. "I can do the hot reading *better* from here," he insisted.

"Are you leaving me to do this show on my own?" Derek sounded incredulous.

"No," Clive said confidently. "I'll be in your ear throughout the evening, and I'll be reading the contents from all the Prayer Messages you've had sent to you."

"You're not fannying around on that Thrill-Kill website, are you?" Derek asked suddenly.

Clive glanced uneasily at the Thrill-Kill login page and scowled at the idea that his brother could sometimes act as though he was genuinely psychic. "You told me to stop visiting that site," Clive reminded Derek. "Do you really think I'm going to disobey one of your explicit instructions?"

"You already read too much about serial killers," Derek complained. "You read about them constantly and then you write about them. And when you're not reading or writing about them, you're talking about them or researching them. I don't want you playing those stupid internet games that glorify those crazy bastards."

"We've had this conversation several times," Clive remembered. "Is there really any purpose to rehashing your thoughts again now that I've said I'll do as you asked?"

Derek was silent for a moment before saying, "This wasn't how we'd agreed to work *Conversations with Dead Friends*, was it? You promised me you'd be with me at the theatre."

"I think this way's better," Clive said earnestly. "There's no one going to see your brother turning up at the theatre and then wonder why he's disappeared whilst you perform. No one's going to find me lurking backstage and whispering information into your earpiece.

This is the perfect cover for *Conversations with Dead Friends*, as well as for the TV idea I gave you yesterday."

"The TV idea?" Derek repeated. There was a moment's silence and Clive knew his brother was struggling to remember what they had discussed. "*Conversations with Dead Serial Killers*?" Derek said eventually. "Is that the TV idea you mean?"

"The title needs a little polish," Clive allowed. "Have you thought any more about it?"

"Not yet," Derek admitted. "I've been busy doing all the solitary preparation for a one-man show. I'd expected some help from my idiot brother but, once again, he's let me down, so I've not had time to think about anything else."

"Perhaps you'll have time tonight, after the show," Clive suggested, ignoring the acid tone and the passive-aggressive comment. "Call me ten minutes before you're going in front of the audience and we'll keep the phone line open for the night."

After severing the connection Clive sat back in his chair and switched on the table lamp next to his desk. It was a lamp he'd made himself with the shade constructed from the face of one of his first victims: Samantha White. Samantha's features turned pale as the bulb cast a pinky-beige light through her stretched cheeks and stitched eyelids. Because her lips had been sealed with clumsy blanket stitches, it looked like she had been caught in the final act of trying to give voice to her dying scream.

Clive grinned at her and typed his details into the login screen of the Thrill-Kill website.